Pest Control

Anton Marks & Akil Hewitt

Marksman Studios
London, United Kingdom

Marksman Studios
www.antonmarks.com

Ordering Information:
Quantity sales. Special discounts are available on quantity purchases by corporations, associations, and others. For details, contact the "Special Sales Department" at the address above.

Pest Control/ Anton Marks & Akil Hewitt -- 1st ed.
ISBN - 978-09562660-9-5

I'm a lazy git, some would say, but I choose to think that I've never found anything that inspires me. I have eclectic tastes. I love astronomy, tech, computers, wild-life, comics, and I'm good at fixing stuff. I have the touch, just not the discipline. So here I am on a chilly West London morning, hustling to my office. Well, office is a loaded word. Before I mislead you into thinking I have a traditional workspace with a desk, swivel chair, filing cabinets, and desktop computer.

Nah!

We call it the Bat Cave as a piss-take because the room is big and only contained a few tables, chairs, a refrigerator, microwave, and a battered big belly TV set. I'm not about to disrespect my humble digs because it comes into its own on mornings like this. I step up the pace, anticipating some warmth from my dodgy electric heater in the Bat Cave, when I see something odd.

It's an orange-red flicker that is pronounced enough to show up against the rising light of the morning. I think it's an electrical spark, arcing between loose wires, something I'd have to report. I hold that idea for a cracked second, just until whatever it is reveals itself to me. A tail swishes, and what looks like limbs flex. One minute it's here, the next it it's gone. The brilliance of it was like someone had let off a noiseless flare and somehow attached it to something living. I shiver; the idea was crazy.

It's not winter just yet, but we are getting some chilly mornings, and although I was made in the UK, I was not built for the UK. Mom's words, not mine.

I've been working here for over three years, so I have a good idea where I saw the spark, and I head towards the source. Spikeway Housing Estate is one of the modern housing complexes in London whose design led the way in contemporary architecture. There are seven apartment buildings set like a heptagon, four, five, and six storeys high with a maximum of thirty residents in each block. Filling the gap between blocks are two to four bedroom homes, so it's a big community. I'm very familiar with how my patch is structured, and I have my scout orienteering badges to prove it, so I head towards Miller House, my eyes peeled on the outside of the building facing me.

I see the flash again. Bright red and orange, a wispy flame in texture that moves along the brickwork like a living thing. It stops, and I could have sworn it ponders its next move before entering Ms. Gerald's flat. Glass explodes outwards and showers the ground below, and I'm looking on with my mouth open.

What did I just see?

I'm no fire expert, but I'm sure a fire doesn't behave like that. I was walking towards it at first, but now I'm running. As soon as I'm below Ms. Gerald's window which is two storeys above me, I look up and watch the double-glazing start to blister - I didn't know glass could do that - then pop. A tongue of flame licks out from the fissure with a scream that makes me question my sanity. I'm sprinting to the main lobby, releasing the fire cabinet, and yanking out the fireman's axe, and I'm taking the stairs two at a time to the second floor.

2.

Heerrrse Johnny!

I shouldn't be grinning, but that blood-curdling catchphrase uttered by the insane Jack Torrance in The Shining just popped into my head. This is serious.

Ms. Gerald could be behind those doors asleep, not knowing her flat is on fire. But how many opportunities would I ever get to smash up Spikeway Housing property without any consequences? The axe feels good in my hand, and I think about my next move carefully. Did I really see what I just saw? Of course, I did. I press ahead, pounding on the green front door and not caring what the neighbors think.

"Ms. Gerald, open up," I holler. "Ms. Gerald, I need you to open this door now."

I'm pounding as I speak, interrupting the racket I'm making by placing my ear to the dusty door to listen for movement inside.

"Ms. Gerald, I'm coming in," I call out again, banging the meaty part of my fist into the wood.

No response.

Hammer time.

I swing the red axe and let it imbed in the area near the handle. I'm handy with it and keep smashing into the door, biting massive chunks of wood as I go. My arms are getting tired, and I have drawn a crowd of neighbors, but I can't stop.

"Can we help, Clayton?" Mr. Longstone in Number 24 asks.

"Call 999," I tell him as I put my shoulder to the ruined door and feel it give.

"She's not in," someone calls out, but I ignore it. I step back and give it the flat of my size elevens, and the door flies open.

Smoke streams out, but not as much as I had

thought. I'm taking no chances. I barge in with my flashlight held up to my chest and head straight for the bedroom. I'm more than familiar with the layout of these units. My heart is pounding, expecting the worst as I burst in.

Empty.

I stare at a neatly made bed and everything in its place. I wheel around, relief making my head hurt, and hustle towards the sitting room.

I look in from the safety of the hallway, covering my nose and mouth with my shirt. Everywhere is dark, obscured by smoke and soot except for one fuzzy ball of intense light and heat. It sits under the twisted flat screen television like the dot at the end of a flaming exclamation mark. Everything around it has been blackened, melted, and scorched but not caught fire. The heat had been too intense, too sudden. I'm scratching my head between coughs, looking at the damage, but my eyes keep coming back to the light source. I point my flashlight directly at it, and the blurry fireball that was beginning to look like something else stirs.

It doesn't like the light. Or was it just me?

It issues an ear-splitting screech that makes me

slap my hand to my ears and step back. Distorted waves of heat ripple off it, then it slivers away. I'm thinking nothing with bone, muscle, and blood could be comfortable in that heat, but it's alive. I'm no David Attenborough, but that is a living thing. Skittering from corner to corner, it melts everything it comes in contact with, and I can feel the heat. It's getting more and more agitated, and it isn't the only one.

You know, how you can feel when the growling dog is readying itself to pounce at you. This is the same but different. I waste no time questioning my instincts. I shuffle behind the door and pull the handle to me just as an explosion of molten spitballs showers the front room like an incendiary barrage from small cannons. It's only when I felt the uncomfortable heat on my skin, the smell of burning wood and the door handle searing my hand that I realize this hiding place is not such a good idea.

I dive to the ground holding my head, rolling behind the sofa and pushing the door shut. My timing is perfect as the door to my earlier safe place is blown off its hinges and flies into the hallway in splinters. I look back, thankful, breathing hard, my heart threatening to jump out of my chest, and the fiery creature nowhere to be seen.

I scramble to my feet, overcome by an existential fear that I have just experienced something inexplicable. If I was smart, I would be calling for help. The fire brigade, my supervisor would have been a good start, but I'm transfixed, not just by what has happened but by an otherworldly vibe that has descended on the scene. When I snap out of my stupor, I look at the damage and moan.

"Oh, man! How the hell am I gonna explain this?"

3.

Ylak Marr woke from the artificial world she inhabited in her induced sleep. It took a minute for her to know who she was and where she was, but as her Seeker instincts kicked into play, she knew something disastrous had happened.

Her kind were able to traverse the vast distances of the galaxy in cryo-sleep, maintaining not just the physical wellbeing of the traveler but also nourishing their active mental processes. Uncle created a mind-scape that was a detailed world in their unconscious that allowed the traveler to live, thrive and even contribute while they slept through light years. Ylak was on an expedition to climb the highest mound on her planet, an honor in her colony, and she was dragged back here into reality.

Looking up at the transparent canopy of her pod, Ylak read the streaming analytics above her, and a picture was beginning to form, as unbelievable as it was. Uncle's memory matrix had booted every system into operation just as she sat up in her crystalline pod, shivering, her senses realigning after periods of suspended animation. Once psychometric liquid blocking her auditory and extrasensory organ leaked out, she not only heard but felt the alarms screaming all across the ship. She needed to know exactly what had happened, and she had to act immediately until Uncle was able.

In moments, she flipped out of her pod, her three bare feet slapping on the cold metal of corridor 1XY. Ylak was moving with intuition. Her first port of call would be the cargo bay and her tiny specimens secured away in their containment cells. On the way, her psionic link with Uncle would kick in and Ylak could have access to the ship's systems. She felt bare and useless without the connection they shared but checking the status of the guests was a priority.

She tried anyway.

"Uncle, are you there?"

There was no response, only static murmuring in the background of her mind as the psionic link to her nervous system remained unconnected.

She'd be lying if she said she wasn't concerned. Ylak was a Seeker, an eon old order that catalogued and established a menagerie of extraordinary lifeforms for study. Pen-67a contained something they had taken extra precautions to secure. And now it was loose. As she hurried through the maze of the ship, she prayed Uncle was okay. He was coming to life nicely. Environmental controls, lighting, antigravity. That was good news. She just wanted to hear his voice.

With so many years of practice, she walked into a vacuum tube, letting the antimatter particles react with the material that made up her flesh and shoot her along its length to a twin juncture. If gravity was at play, she would say she was going down. But out here in space, the concept of up and down meant nothing. She stepped into the habitation hold and could only stare at the devastation in disbelief.

"No! No! No!"

Portions of the hull had been breached, and Uncle

had resealed the damaged areas in autonomous mode. Most of the destruction was focused in the specimen zone for the Nova-001X, acquired from the jungle planet Sigma Minor in the Lekcom star system. The tendrils along Ylak's central spine stood on end as she recalled first contact with the species she called the Omni-Seed. They had only stopped there for the rare deposits of Taconium but were kept in survival mode the entire three revolutions as the jungle planet actively tried to eliminate her.

At first, they thought they had been plagued by a set of unfortunate circumstances until Uncle quickly surmised it was intelligent orchestration - in other words, the attacks were controlled. From Uncle's initial analysis of the planet, it seemed it had no civilization. It was later on that the sentient computer discovered that wasn't quite right. The society that had come before had been wiped from the face of the planet.

Ylak never did find out why the Omni-Seed had such an overwhelming desire to destroy her. What she did know was the malice shown to her was also the undoing of any intelligent lifeforms with ambitions to elevate themselves from fire to plasma drives. Ylak would leave that conclusion to the Conclave scientists to discover. All she knew was, at the time, it took Uncle's substantial computing power to pinpoint the location of the Omni-Seed controlling that region of the planet.

Fortune had stepped in next when she had used a flock of winged creatures that didn't seem to be under its control but who had an uncanny talent for vocal mimicry and were unusually gregarious. Ylak hatched a plan of shielding herself amongst the friendly flying vocalists, giving her the ability to get close to the Omni-Seed without being detected. They never discovered why these creatures were immune to the Omni-Seed's influence. In minutes she had it neutralized and on its way to Uncle in a containment pod. It felt like a lifetime ago but look where she was now. Another planet and another fight for survival.

She had never seen such a keen sense of survival in a living thing, especially one that relied on symbiotic relationships for most aspects of its survival. Ylak shook off the memory and looked at the damage again, baffled at how it had managed to sabotage their ship, escape its confines and shoot itself to the habitable planet they were orbiting. Uncle was still not talking to her, but his diagnostic capabilities were nearly fully functional. The bad news was being fed directly to her. And yes, it was as bad, if not worse than she thought.

4.

The news of this morning's fire and my heroics spread to most of the estate. I'm trying to ignore it because I have a massive clean-up job ahead of me. For some reason, last night had been crazy busy on the estate and the detritus left behind from whatever happened requires my attention. The distraction is good but is punctuated by residents wanting to fill in the gaps to this morning's incident. Ms. Roberts, walking her dog, must have thought I was Superman.

"Breaking down doors to save the day, you'll be leaping tall buildings in a single bound next," the middle-aged woman grins, pulling at the leash of her over-excited terrier. "I'm glad you're on our side, Clayton," she looks me up and down. "Have you been working out?"

"Just my usual," I say, but her legs are already in second gear and moving away from me.

"No drugs, those steroids aren't good for you. You know that, right?"

I nod and raise my voice because she's pulling away quickly.

"I don't do drugs, Ms. Roberts, and I…"

Before I can explain my stance on drug use, she is dragged away by her dog, which I think must be the one on steroids because the little mutt shouldn't be able to pull its owner like that. She is still talking but has been dragged out of earshot. I shrug and try to get back to work. No such luck. As soon as I turn the corner on Poseidon House, I'm mugged by the yummy mummies going to Yoga class.

"Namaste."

I can never tell if they are taking the piss when they greet me like that, but this morning, I'm grateful for their kind words as they thank me for my service. I want to tell them it's my job, but I don't want to seem as if I can't take a compliment. I thank them, my head already two sizes bigger than normal, and head for the Bat Cave, thinking I need a pair of dark glasses and a baseball cap to get me through the rest of the day.

I'm showing off, of course.

I really do appreciate the love being directed my way; it's just that I'm still working out what I saw in Ms. Gerald's flat and how I was meant to position that in my head. From my experience of being an employee of Spikeway Housing Estate, the investigation will be uncomfortable. Just the thought of talking to management has me feeling apprehensive. I'm still not sure how I'm going to spin the facts. I need to share my concerns with someone, but how do I do that without them looking at me strangely.

Dad is a good listener, but I know he will laugh and say I'm seeing things. His closing comments would be, 'Son, you have an issue with authority, and you are not fulfilling your potential, but you're a big man. You've made your bed, now lie in it.'

And he would be kinda right. I like to be left alone and being in the great outdoors with the ability to use my initiative without being micromanaged is perfect for me. Okay, the money isn't great, but I live with my parents for now anyway, so I'm good. And I mean to keep it that way. I don't want to be fired or sectioned in this impending meeting. I plan on telling them what they want to hear.

That is a worry for another time; right now, I switch my focus to what went on last night. I'm heading towards the Bat Cave for some supplies after Laura at the reception desk gave me a list of work I need to look at.

Over fifteen calls had been made, ranging from suspected vandalism to noise complaints. This morning, calls came in from residents reporting damage to cars, buildings, trees and the grounds of the park. What the hell had happened? I have a lot to go through on top of my own duties but decide to ease myself into my day by tackling the mystery of the Vandalized Rubbish Receptacle first. Although I suspect vandalism is a strong word for a few drunken squiggly marks with spray paint or a marker, I would go and see for myself.

I'm lucky this estate has only a few hardcore elements to deal with. The Spikeway Housing Association keeps a tight ship, and because management don't have the experience of dealing with bad situations, they tend to exaggerate their severity. With that being said, last night was unusual, an aberration. So, imagine my delight when I walk into the community center, saunter across the shiny auditorium floor to the back of house and push open the door to the Bat Cave to see my partner in crime who had been on holiday, his back to me, his headphones on, and his feet up.

I pick up a roll of toilet paper and slather a generous helping of hand sanitiser all over its surface, then sneak up behind him. Laughter threatens to burst from my lips as I launch it straight at his head. It hits him on the temple, sticks to his skin for a moment before rolling to the floor. He flounders comically on his chair, nearly falling off, then scrapes at his face with disgust and panic; his lizard brain is telling him something nasty was on his cheek. I'm rolling on the floor, my eyes watering as I exploit his squeamish nature, but I couldn't help myself. I missed him.

Momentary confusion gives way to recognition, and a broad, relieved smile plasters on his face.

"You're a wanker," Steven Cooper says, jumping up from his chair to greet me.

"Of course, I am, you lazy git," I say, laughing. "How was your holiday?"

It's a stupid question; the man has something as close to a tan as his skin would permit.

"Classic," he says. "Sun, sea, and food, mate. I didn't have to lift a finger."

"So, it was a bit like work then," I say.

"Har-di-har. I do my fair share."

"I know you do, mate," I pause and grin at him. "In your dreams."

"If that's how you feel, then I can leave you to it and go home for a snooze."

"Nice try," I say, getting into his personal space with a bear hug. "It's good having you back, but some of us have to work for a living."

We unclench, and I punch him on his shoulder.

"I've got pics," Steven raises his voice and shakes his phone suggestively.

"Beach?" I ask.

"Clayton, come on, man. It's me you're talking to."

Yeah, that was another stupid question to ask. London-born Steven is a sun seeker. He would never travel to a country that isn't hot or doesn't have a beach, although his ancestors came from the Outer Hebrides. Wiry, ruddy cheeked and with a neat beard that he treasures. Running the estate would be so much more difficult without his easy-going presence.

"Clean up your dick pics and I'll look at your shots, lunchtime. I've got stuff to do, and so do you."

"Need a third leg?" Steven asks.

I shake my head confused and smile again.

"So, I can do all the work while you watch? No, thank you."

"Oh, ye of little faith."

"Divide and conquer today, mate. We've got a full day. Check the clipboard and pick a number, any number."

Steven sighs.

I grab solvents, a bucket, a sponge, and a cloth. I make my way out.

5.

It was one revolution of the planet below them since Ylak had been awakened from cryo-sleep with her ship damaged and a dangerous lifeform escaping its confinement and departing the starship. Ylak was slowly piecing together what had happened, but she was having trouble believing the evidence. Uncle had his voice back, and as he explained their predicament from the available data, he began repairing himself.

"This will not do; this will not do!" Uncle lamented.

"We underestimated it," Ylak said.

"We did, little one," Uncle said. "That we did, but never again. Never!"

"Never! I shouldn't be surprised by any of this. I should have listened."

"Yes, you should have, but not for the reasons you think," Uncle said. "Our relationship works because we are learning from each other. My bio-quantum networks strive to be more...emotional, and you strive to be more logical."

Ylak blinked twice in agreement.

"We both saw the threat. My systems wanted organism Nova-001X chemically subdued. You reasoned that a sentient being should be allowed some freedom in a controlled environment. You were wrong, and logic should have taken precedence. I process and improve; you process and learn. Remember, no recriminations, little one. I will not have that."

Ylak should have realized her AI companion would not want her assigning blame on an event they should both learn from. Ylak was already far along into that process.

"What did you learn from Nova-001X while I slept?" Ylak's three optical receptors seemed to consider something. "Can we call it by its designation Omni-Seed?

"Of course." Uncle agreed.

"What do you need to know?"

"How? How did it bypass your systems? How did it escape the pen and leave the starship?"

"I'm beginning to understand how it managed to be at the top of the food chain. It's cunning. A description I would use for hunting predators but applies two-fold to the Omni-Seed. It is a perfectly evolved organism. It was in a dormant state for some time but must have become active as soon as my systems went into standby mode. It was learning all it could from my network. It was tapping into my Quantum systems. A being with no means of locomotion, and yet it psionically commandeered insects that are resident in the cargo hold to release the higher order species that use tools in their habitat. These species, mainly tetrapod's and tripodal creatures, were taught how to release it from bondage. The Omni-Seed increased their intelligence as and when it needed to and genetically modified them on a cellular level when it was done. The zombie creatures then jammed up our star drive systems with their dead bodies. I became aware immediately, but not before my emergency protocols released an airlock for engineer EVA."

"I'm your engineer," Ylak said, upset with the Omni-Seed's presumption.

"You are," Uncle teased. "And an admirable one for an organic lifeform."

Air whistled through Ylak's breathing flutes with musical notes of amusement.

"It played you like a grandmaster of Kraxian Chess, Uncle. Will you study it or marry it?"

The sentient starship paused.

"If I knew that I had to deal with your annoying and juvenile attempts at RocTaa, I would have left you in cryo-sleep."

"You know you'd miss my company," Ylak said. "And you're going to need me for this. So where are we?"

"Let's work while we talk," Uncle said.

"Are you trying to imply I'm not working hard enough?" Ylak asked.

"You, my little one, have no true concept of the term hard work." The voice in her head paused. "To answer your first question. My astronomical charts say we were forced out of a wormhole cluster that services this sector of space. We are in orbit around the only planet in the star system with higher lifeforms who have established rudimentary civilization. The planet is designated Epsilon."

"Epsilon?" Ylak repeated quietly. "It's going to destroy them, Uncle. I can't let that happen."

"We can't let this happen," Uncle emphasized.

"They're infants," Ylak bemoaned. "They haven't had manned missions beyond their own solar system. They've had no contact with other intelligent lifeforms outside of their planet."

"Correct," Uncle said. "Personally, I would prefer contact with the ocean dwelling Whale and Octopus species of the planet. Unfortunately, their evolutionary path took them elsewhere. Instead, we have to contend with the land-dwelling Homo sapiens."

"Bipedal, oxygen breathers," Ylak added.

"Amongst other things," Uncle said. "My scans of their media say out of seven point eighty-nine billion people on the planet, four point twenty-four billion think they are alone in the universe."

Ylak groaned.

"What chance do they have?"

"None," Uncle said. "Civilization as they know it will end. These humans are a resilient species, but watching it come to ruin before its time is not acceptable, especially if we had a hand in its demise. We must intervene."

"I agree. What do you want from me?"

A line of silence connected both brain and Quantum computer for a moment. Then Uncle went on.

"I have taken the time to begin code knitting your human impulses, human idiosyncrasies, memory, emotion, vocalization, bipedalism, etcetera into a human consciousness algorithm that I will implant in your neural substrate. Their brains are very complex, it's a shame they use so little of it, but I will have it ready using all my resources. You will also have the option to choose your human form which will be a flawless combination of Dyanco and Ityfa mimicry technology."

"Will the transplant hurt?" Ylak asked.

"It will, but just for the procedure. You'll be fine. You were bred for this."

There was no need for confirmation. Ylak trusted

him with her life.

They were connected ever since she was hatched, organic and Mechano-organic.

"I need to repair myself, create your consciousness and your new body" Uncle said. "And you have twenty-four Earth hours to prepare for the shift."

"Do you remember how many times I came close to expiration, tracking and capturing that thing?" Ylak asked.

"I do," Uncle said. "I forget nothing, remember."

Ylak whistled in amusement.

"Don't you know there is no one better suited in this sector to do this than you," Uncle said. "The Omni-Seed may be dangerous and smart, but you are smarter. We are a team, little one, and together we can retrieve it before it destroys these lifeforms."

"Where on the planet did the capsule crash-land?" Ylak asked casually.

"I have pinpointed the beacons position in the metropolis of London on the landmass of the United Kingdom."

6.

I'm heading towards my clean-up job, and in the moments between the Bat Cave and that exciting prospect, my mind flashes back to what I saw this morning. Or what I thought I saw. My mind is dredging up staccato snapshots of a creature within the flames. A creature that wanted to fry my arse. I snap out of the memory, shivering. The jury's still out on whether I was going crazy or not. What I do know is I have a feeling that something has shifted for me, something that could change everything.

Shock?

Maybe. It's just made me start reflecting on my place in the world. Deep for this time of day. Not uncommon for me. The last time I was thinking like this, I took an Open University course in Pest Control a year ago and received a qualification. I couldn't bring myself to tell my mom and dad, not yet. That milestone felt good; the sense of achievement kick-started something in me, and I started discovering some interesting things about myself. It turns out I'm a natural around scientific concepts and I'm good at anticipating and solving problems. I wonder what this new episode is going to reveal about myself. I have to wait and see.

As soon as I arrive at the refuge area, I'm struck with a sense of strangeness that has gooseflesh erupting on the back of my neck and my arms. I stand there looking at the scene, knowing it hasn't been interfered with since last night. About thirty empty cans of lager are set in a neat pattern around the refuge container. My eyes pick up a cluster of mice droppings around a set of cracks in the concrete that weren't there four days ago. They are fresh and so are the cracks.

My focus shifts to the intricate multicolored chalk markings of a kind that make it look like mystical mandala patterns scratched on the floor of an urban temple. The big refuge container, set perfectly in the middle of this work of spontaneous abstract art, is tattooed with something even more tribal. I'm not prepared for how beautiful and intricate this supposed act of vandalism is. I immediately start to doubt whether this had been rendered by Percival Owens, the estate drunk.

This couldn't have been one night's work. How could the culprit see in the dark to do this anyway? I move a bit closer to observe the detailed chalk drawings surrounding the refuge container. I was honestly expecting a level of creativity that straddled obscene, ridiculous, or bland. This is exquisite and intriguing. I didn't know Percy had it in him, and I guess I was wrong. Standing amongst beer cans and discarded chalk, I walk around the container as the images tell a story.

I look at something that resembled a satellite or spaceship, a constellation all around, then a shower of falling stars landing amongst houses and buildings. But in the middle of all that is an oval light or power source radiating energy outwards. There are stick people on the ground, and around them are some strange animals roaming freely through the buildings. It's an arresting image and very creepy as my eyes slide over the details. I take out my smartphone and snap a shot. I think of posting it but decide against it. I want to keep this to myself for now. I snap on my rubber gloves, spray some solvent over the area and put some elbow grease into removing it.

I know I have to remove it, but I feel guilty for every stroke that wipes away the urban masterpiece. I scrub away the last remnants from this mysterious art attack and decide to find the only man I know with a drinking problem and artistic pretensions. When you work somewhere like this long enough, you can't help but meet some larger-than-life personalities. Percy is one such tenant. He could make more friends in a state of inebriation than he ever could when sober. And the tenants love him. He is a kind soul whose demons he feels can only be controlled with the aid of drink.

I find Percy sleeping in The Cell, an area that was once the storage nook for a petrol lawnmower but was abandoned when the lawnmower's gas-guzzling days ended, and rechargeable mowers replaced it. Management don't seem to know what to do with it. They removed the grilled security door that kept out trespassers but never replaced it. The whole section looks like a prison cell a drugged-out architect mistakenly added to his drawings. It's attached to the building Percy resides in and has an uninterrupted view of the garden, with only one point of access through the parking bays.

Percy sits precariously on a chair that he must have grabbed out of his studio flat and plonked outside. He is asleep, performing an amazing feat of balance as the chair rocks from four legs to two without a hint of him falling on his arse. I almost don't want to wake him, but I have to warn him about the drawings. I should talk to him and keep it between us, keeping the Housing Committee out of it. I come up close, and once he has four chair legs on the ground, I poke him.

"Percy, Percy! Wake up, man."

It takes two more jabs to rouse him with a snort and flaying of arms as he returns to the land of the living. Percy's eyes gain focus, and it looks like this is one of the rare occasions I have caught him sober. He smiles when he recognizes me.

"Enjoying the shade?" I ask him.

He stretches, makes a groaning sound, and I hear

a pop of joints clicking in place.

"Wonderful."

I wish I could be as carefree as he is. No job, no family, wherever you lay your hat is your home lifestyle. I feel like a party crasher, but rules are rules.

"It wouldn't have been so wonderful if someone else other than me had seen your artwork on the big metal wheelie bin."

"What artwork?" Percy asks.

"Don't tell me you can't remember."

Percy shrugs.

He reaches down, scratches his balls, picks up a thermos, unscrews the top, and pours himself coffee I can smell from where I stand.

"These are yours, aren't they?" I hand him ten sticks of colored chalk. His eyes shine with recognition.

"Oh man, I must have had a skin full. I didn't draw anything pornographic, did I?"

"It was beautiful, actually. A shame I had to clean it," I say.

"A fan," Percy claps his hands together with excitement. "I haven't had admirers of my work since uni."

I shake my head.

"Trust me, you don't want the other type of admirers your work could have attracted; they wouldn't be as nice." I lower my voice and stare at him intently. "You've got to stop doing this, Percy, or you could lose your accommodation. Do you understand what I'm trying to say?"

Percy drops his head, considering my words. What do I expect him to say? That he is going to give up drinking. That he'll be a better citizen. It would take much more than good intentions on my part for that to happen. He lifts his head and looks at me.

"I was inside," Percy says. "I had a few brews, then I saw the light show through the windows."

"Light show?" I ask.

He continues.

"It was in the sky, like a meteor shower and lightning storm all rolled into one." His voice dips as he thinks about it, then his eyes shift as he tries to recover a fleeting memory.

"The TV was on, and I was watching a documentary on jazz in New Orleans."

I'm listening to him carefully, trying to make a connection with his drawings and his account of what he remembers. Something on the edge of my awareness is about to tip over into recollection, but not just yet. I let it go for now.

"I remember looking at the captivating light and then…and then…"

His brow crunches; he looks at the ground, at his hands, then at his feet again, not meeting my eyes.

He goes on.

"There was an explosion in the grounds, like a piece of the firmament broke off from the heavens," Percy smiles at his poetic flourish. "I can't remember much after that. Flashes of memory altered states, crappy weird visions."

I know this is going from vandalism to psychedelia, but I have to ask him.

"Have you ever had visions like that before?"

His answer is immediate.

"Never." He shoots me a toothy grin. "Whatever was in those beers, the hangover was truly epic."

"Did you smoke a spliff with all that?" I ask.

"How dare you! My body is a temple," Percy

laughs. “I don’t do drugs.”

“Right,” I say. I guess we all have our standards.

“Last night was a crazy one for everybody, it seems, but you’ve just got to be careful. They’re watching.”

“Let them watch,” Percy sounds circumspect. “What will be, will be.”

I can see he means it.

Percy reminds me of the ancient Stoics I like reading about who weren’t afraid of meeting what life threw at them head-on. There could be something to that.

“You know I’m on your side, right?” I say to him.

“I appreciate it, brother.” Percy looks more awake than he had throughout our conversation. “Everybody needs that sometimes.”

“Yes, we do,” I say. “Yes, we do.”

7.

All the way back to the Bat Cave, I'm replaying Percy's words in my head and trying to understand the image he drew on the giant trashcan. What really held my attention was the meteor shower he had been talking about. Why had it stuck like a piece of spinach in my teeth? I'm not really sure. I have always had a thing for astronomy; I own a cool Stargazer 2000 telescope at home and a bookshelf filled with books on astronomy, popular science, pest control, music, and a bunch of my favorite speculative fiction authors. It would have been interesting if I could confirm the event with other stargazers online.

You can tell I'm not a regular on the astronomy

message boards because I should have known if there was any significant galactic activity last night. It would have to be as spectacular as Percy made it out to be. London's light pollution is extensive, so seeing astronomical phenomena in the night sky is difficult depending on where you live. Anything that could pierce the veil produced by the capital's constant drive to be a genuinely twenty-four hour city must be significant.

So now you also know I'm a bit of a nerd. Not that it has anything to do with anything. It just feels like it should be significant, I don't know why. All I know is, it's given me a funny feeling of purpose. Making my workday that little bit more interesting.

With that thought, I push through the community center's swing doors and head to the Bat Cave. I can see the door has been left ajar as I approach, and my happy-go-lucky mood dissipates. Steven knows I have a thing about pulling doors shut, and he is in the habit of doing it after months of training. Anyway, he couldn't have finished his job so quickly. I slowly push the door open and step inside. Standing over my desk with his back to me is my line manager, Duncan Riley. He turns when he hears me come in.

"Mr. French, I'm glad you made it back," he smiles. His dress jacket is buttoned in the middle smartly, white shirt and tie neat as usual. It's a pity about the uncontrollable explosion of sandy hair on the top of his head. "I had a gap in my schedule today, so I decided we could talk. Your incident this morning requires a swift resolution, Mr. French." He makes that sound like a threat.

My incident? I think. I've just saved your bosses a significant bill for extensive property damage. You're welcome.

"You haven't got any jobs that are urgent, have you?" he asks.

A trick question. I know he is trying to stir up shit, and I let him. We are supposed to record our jobs on a work intranet before we tackle them. We both know the procedure. I look at him and say nothing, waiting for him to reveal what I already know about him.

"I checked it anyway," he says, smiling condescendingly. "We can do this."

"No problem," I reply, grimacing. "What do you need from me?"

Duncan opens his leather case on my desk and fishes out an incident form. He hands it to me.

“Fill it out, and we can talk when you’re done. Answer all the questions.”

I groan inwardly and reach for my pen.

* * *

I should have left that interview with bruises all over my body; that’s how painful it was. I’ve never stepped foot in a police station in my life, but I would imagine the interview technique I just experienced is similar. I thought only my mom had mastered those inquisition techniques. I should have known better. Making you leave a discussion feeling guilty but knowing you are innocent is a skill. I decide I’ve given gingerbread man enough of my energy. I have other things on my mind. Percy has me thinking about the astronomical phenomena, especially the throwaway comment about debris crashing into the estate.

A piece of the firmament broke off from the heavens, is what Percy said. Am I sad for looking for excitement? I’m not saying my job is completely devoid of novelty, but it could do with some more adventure. And who would turn up their nose to adventure? I leave the Bat Cave before Steven returns from his second job of the day - the inspection of a merry-go-round - and promise myself I'll give him a call on the radio in a minute. I may even see him when I do my rounds. I just won't let him know what I'm up to. Not just yet.

8.

"Explosions! Yes, I heard explosions? How did you know?" Mr. Singh responds excitedly.

Mr. Malik Singh is one of the coolest Uber drivers I know. He lives with his wife - his kids are all grown up - and always has the most delicious Indian sweets in his pantry.

"It must be some kids playing around with fireworks, I suppose," Malik says. "You know us Sikhs love a good party."

I smile and nod in agreement.

"What did you see outside?" I let the question slide over to him, hoping his recollection matches Percy's accounts. They do, but try as I may, I've come across no firework debris as evidence.

"You know what was strange, though?" He pauses to think.

I lean in closer. Mr. Singh is good at weaving a tale, even with the meager plot elements he has at his disposal.

"There were about three or four explosions that lit up the night sky, and then nothing."

"No lights, no smoke?" I interrupt.

"No, I don't mean like that," he says. "It was like the sound outside had been sucked away. You know that background sound of the city that we're so used to that we don't notice it until it's gone."

I nod.

"I remember trying to clear my ears with a yawn. You know the way you would on a flight, but it wasn't me; it was outside. Then after a bit, I heard a car horn, and the sounds kinda returned. It was okay again. I went back to watching Top Gear."

"Thanks for the heads up, Mr. S. The Association is always concerned about the residents' safety." I sound like a promotional pamphlet, but I need to make this seem like a company thing.

"I almost forgot," Mr. Singh says, disappearing

into his apartment. He returns with a small box that he hands to me. "Your favorites."

I shake the box, knowing they are filled with the sweets I love.

"You know this could be considered bribery of an association employee?"

Mr. Singh grins and shrugs.

"I will take my chances."

The next day, I swing by Mr. Singh's place, still unsure where I'm going with all this, but I'm glad I did. The excitement of yesterday seems to have calmed down as no one else is bending my ear. I'm on my break, and I head for what, to my mind, is the best place to start my investigation. At least the most picturesque. I walk up to the fenced area of play equipment and artificial landscape with a ten-foot-tall rock feature stuck at one end. It's about an acre in dimension and used by dog owners, bored kids, and smokers.

I walk through one of the five gates surrounding the area which allows easy access, heading to the focal point. The landscape designer who created this little oasis amidst the concrete had left his own three-dimensional signature on his work. The cube that was part metal and part concrete looks as if a giant toddler rammed one of its corners into the ground and waddled off, leaving it wedged in place. It'sa fantastic background for a selfie, and an unlicensed climbing frame for some of the more adventurous kids.

That is my starting point as I circumvent the park, ending right where I began. I haven't a clue what I'm looking for. What would be cool would be a meteorite fragment, but discarded fireworks would explain a lot too.

There is nothing. No debris and no impact marks.

I suddenly stop in my tracks, and for a moment, I'm back in Ms. Geralds flat. I'm sweating. The heat is relentless, the otherworldly silhouette moving like a lizard within the flames is hissing and spitting its molten venom.

The memory recedes, but I'm still breathing hard and shivering on the spot. When I gather my wits, I'm left with the chilling conclusion and an accompanying sinking feeling that all this is related somehow. The lights in the sky, the explosions, the meteor shower, the weird drawings on the bin, and my close encounter of the strange kind. I just don't know how.

Twenty minutes into my walkabout and I've discovered nothing more interesting than scattered nitrogen capsules, a newspaper, and a liter bottle of what could be cider but I suspect is piss stood on its bottom refracting sunlight onto the grass. My mind wanders a bit because I'm getting hungry. Mom is making my favorite style of shepherd's pie this evening, and I'm conjuring up its look and smell. I catch myself salivating. It's not a good look.

That's when I see her.

She is kneeling beside a set of workout equipment. The mystery woman is in grey coveralls, her head is lowered to the ground, and she has dark caramel skin - I can see her hands and shoulder-length kinky brown hair. My inquisitiveness gets the better of me, and I walk up and stand beside her, but she's so engrossed with what she is doing, she doesn't notice me. After a few seconds of being ignored, I decide to intervene; she's in my 'hood' after all. I know I may sound like a jobsworth, but I need to know any company working on the estate and make sure they have the correct paperwork.

In truth, a supervisor should be doing this, but since the last estate supervisor left, they haven't filled the position. Obviously, I wasn't in the running, or I'm not supervisor material in their eyes. Maybe if I had put myself forward, but it wouldn't have been the right thing for me, I know that now. Still, the buck stops with me, and after the horrors of recent tower block fires, I do my best to follow the regs, question anything I'm not sure of, and cover my arse for blow-back.

"How's it going?" I ask.

The woman stops whatever she is doing, hesitates, and then turns her head towards me. The movement is elegant and very controlled, like it had been practiced and executed to perfection.

Something about her strikes me hard, and the words catch in my throat. I don't usually get tongue-tied around attractive women, even ones with flawless skin, high cheeks, deep brown sparkling eyes, and lips inherited from her African or Caribbean roots. She tied her unruly curls with an elasticated band of red, green, and black.

Her image shimmers for a second, and I blink to clear my vision. I catch myself holding my breath, and before I give myself brain damage, I forget everything I was about to say. In an ideal world, it would have been witty and charming, but it has slivered away like an eel. She looks me up and down, and I'm guessing she's unimpressed by the green uniform. For a moment, her scrutiny feels like an analysis.

Cold and calculating.

In a beat, her composure changes, and she quickly puts away the piece of flashing equipment she has in her hand and stands up to face me.

She smiles for the first time.

"You must be Clayton French? I'm Nikki Turnbull. Nikki with a double 'k.' Pleased to meet you."

She shoots out a hand that I take and then nearly forget to shake.

Her hand is soft, her approach is awkward but warm.

"This is going to sound stupid," I say. "But I don't know who you are."

She shakes her head.

"Your managers didn't let you know?"

I shake my head.

Nikki sighs.

"I'm a post-grad student for the Urban Zoology department at the University of Greenwich. We're doing a month-long research project into the mice, rats, and bats population here. I have got all the paperwork if you want to see it."

"Nah!" I say much too quickly. "I will contact my line manager and get all the details from him."

Reading the boring legalese these documents generated is not my idea of a fun read. Nikki is more interesting.

"They must be happy with the paperwork, or they'd let me know." I pause, feeling I have already taken up enough of her time. I'm considering how I should excuse myself from our little encounter. I definitely don't want to go, but it looks like she has important work to do.

Come to think of it, I've got work to do too.

Before I can clumsily say anything, Nikki says, "I'll...see you around, Clayton."

"Yeah, definitely. I'm hard to miss." I point to the garish green uniform I'm wearing, and she laughs.

9.

Later that night, train driver Andrew Faulkner looked out from his second floor flat with a broad grin on his face. He loved the idea of being able to look down from any window of his apartment and see his hybrid silver Mercedes parked in its cozy space. It was apparent he had a passion for the machine because his love affair with it had not depreciated after years of ownership. This was a typical early shift. His phone alarm woke him, and he padded into the lounge, parted the curtains with his finger to see his baby sat all pretty and sleek in the forecourt.

Andrew went through his usual ablutions and was ready for work in forty-five minutes flat, shaving off five minutes on his regular time. He didn't eat this early in the morning but had his morning coffee black and aromatic with a spoon of grass-fed butter. Andrew was ready to take on any challenges his train could throw at him.

Closing his front door, he whistled an old school R&B tune and then remembered he needed to report a missing fire extinguisher from the lobby to the super, Clayton. He took the stairs down to the ground floor, a slight edge of tiredness disappearing as soon as he opened the lobby door and the brisk morning air slapped his cheeks. Usually, Andrew would remotely disengage the car's locking system as he approached it, and the silver beast would make its characteristic bleep, bleep sound. Not this morning.

He tried again.

No response.

By this time, he was standing beside it, wondering when he would get the time to drop it off at his car dealership. Andrew used his key to open the door, an unusual action for him, and slipped into the comfort of his car.

Key in, ignition on.

Nothing happened.

Andrew's smile was still there, but it was fading fast.

He turned the key again, and an electronic murmur would have been appreciated, but it was non-responsive.

He slammed the back of his head on the headrest in frustration, and that's when he heard the faint sound. He had to keep his eyes closed, but a rhythmic scratching sound persisted. Andrew perked up and tried to follow the source of the muffled sounds. After a few moments of detective work, he concluded it was coming from the engine. Just before he called work to tell them he'd be late, he would investigate. Check out what had gone wrong.

Stepping out of the car, he started wondering if this was malicious. That toe-rag from Number 40 still carried a grudge after Andrew confronted him about his four-legged twin shitting in the grass strips between parking spaces. He better not have. That would be overstepping the mark.

Andrew moved to the front of the Mercedes and placed his palm on the bonnet. It was warm, although he had shut off the engine over twelve hours ago. The metronomic tik-tik of metals contracting continued, louder and more persistent.

There were two modes of accessing the engine. Andrew snaked his fingers between the radiator and the lip of the hood, felt the spring-loaded metal bolt, and depressed, levering it up. The engine compartment was a pool of darkness, and nothing of its components was distinguishable. It was like a liquid shadow had been poured into the cavity. Andrew's heart hammered in his chest; his common sense was being overridden by his primitive early warning system.

His hands shaking, he felt in his pockets for his smartphone and switched on his flashlight app. He waved the phone over the engine, and something black, thick, and serpentine was coiled around the engine block. Andrew let out a wheezy yelp and stepped back. Whatever it was tightened its grip on the engine, surprised by the invasion. Blood drained from Andrew's face. One step backward became two, and then an awkward stumble. He drew air into his lungs with the intent of letting it out in a scream. He never managed it.

A whip-like protuberance shot out from the engine cavity, licked the air, and encircled his throat. Both his hands came up to grab at the clammy and disgustingly spongy noose that was pulling him towards the car. His phone fell out of his pocket as he shook his head wildly, desperate to get loose. All he could muster was a breathing reprieve as another octopus-like extension shot into his mouth, cutting off his breathing with a strangled Urk!

A bitter, prickly sensation exploded in his mouth; his mind processed the horror being fed down his throat through his bulging eyes as he was pulled headfirst into the engine with the sound of a melon bursting. His body thrashed as dying nerve impulses fired signals to appendages that would soon come to realize their central command was smashed out of his skull and dripping on the tarmac. The sound of the engine or what was a horrific reproduction of it started up, and the remainder of Andrew Faulkner was fed into the engine like a meat grinder. When it was done, the bonnet slammed shut.

10.

One of the biggest mistakes I made when I started working here is telling residents that home for me is a fifteen-minute bus ride away. Some, not all, think I'm on twenty-four hours call, seven days a week like a genie. And the company's website doesn't help discourage that kind of misinformation.

You are never on your own. Call us twenty-four hours a day, and a friendly Spikeway Housing staff member will be there for you.

Who came up with these lines?

The truth is I'm on call only twice a week, and the only time I would appear after work hours is in the case of an emergency. My heroics three days ago at Ms. Gerald's apartment didn't help my case either.

Clayton French, he'll be there for you no matter what!

Not what I want to be known for, but it looks like I'm going to be stuck with it.

I've been home nearly five hours now. I kissed Mom on the cheek, ignoring her protests of picking up the trainers I left on entry and lamenting about past indiscretions, asking me in the same breath whether I thought she was my slave. I love that Jamaican woman. She may be a misery guts sometimes, but I couldn't live without her. And yes, she is practically my slave.

I showered while mom was in the kitchen. In moments, I was fresh and squeaky clean, in sweats and retiring to my room for a night of Google research. The mystery of what happened three nights ago would not solve itself. I share a room with my younger brother. He is mostly into music, and I'm not sure what I'm into. I know I should have my own space, but this is London. On my salary, forget it. Where could I go and get a roof over my head with a home-cooked meal every evening? Speaking about a home-cooked meal, dinner is nearly ready. I know this because I keep asking, and that's when my mobile starts vibrating.

I pick up on the third ring.

A fatal mistake.

The voice is frantic, but it still manages to make my heart hitch.

It's the seductive voice of Ms. Richardson.

She's the beautiful single mom of a five-year-old who lives in Hamilton House. The one I gave my personal number to. If I was honest, it was bullshit. I gave it to her on the pretense of a concerned caretaker. If she had any issues, she could give good old Clayton a call. But the real reason, and I thought she knew it too, was having a direct line for a hookup if the spirit moved her. My little ploy has worked, but I have a feeling a booty call would not be the outcome.

"Hey, Maggie, how you doing?" I say. She always insisted I call her by her first name.

"Clayton!" she answers, her voice a harsh whisper. "Clayton!" The urgency in her voice makes popping sounds as she breathes.

"Are you all right?" I ask with a calm concern that is slowly becoming ice-cold terror.

"There's...something in the flat with me," she says, her voice tremulous.

"Something like what?" I ask.

"I don't know," she whispers. "Me and Zak are locked in the bedroom. I saw it just after I started washing up the plates. The front door's still open. Whatever it is, it likes my kitchen. I didn't know who else to call. I didn't know who else."

Her plea strokes my ego, and that's all I need.

"I'll come right over. Stay in your bedroom," I say.

"Please hurry." The cold fingers of creeping panic in her voice reach out to me through the connection.

Twenty-five minutes later, I'm standing at 115 Hamilton House, gripping my dad's tool kit. I start wondering how I'm gonna gain access, and I immediately flashback to Mrs. Gerald's flat and my fireman routine. Thankfully, I'm spared another management interview as the front door is open. I put the tool pan down to block the door from closing and take a cursory look inside. I reach for my dad's mini crowbar, twirl it over my fingers like a boss, and walk inside.

"Maggie!" I call. "Maggie, you all right?"

A muffled voice from upstairs answers me. I can

feel the relief in her voice from down here.

"We're fine," she calls out. "It's in the kitchen."

I groan inwardly, hoping there is no need for me to do any investigation, just rescue the damsel in distress.

The kitchen.

The apartment is small and well-lit. Stairs to the two rooms upstairs are in front of the door, and the kitchen, which is roomy for this size of the apartment, is just on the right. Light from the short hallway illuminates it, and I make a cursory look inside. I'm expecting a fox or a rat; what else could it be?

What else indeed.

I swing the crowbar forward before I take a step into the kitchen. I feel for the light switch, flick it on and start looking for would-be intruders. There are three plates in the sink, the countertop is clean, and there is a small table near the entrance with magazines, cookbooks, and a notepad. I turned around and look down to see a shattered glass jar on the floor and pasta scattered everywhere. The smell of cinnamon hangs in the air. I stoop to get a better look at what could be under the table, but it's organized and clean. I reach out to touch a see-through plastic box filled with nic-nacs when I hear a rapid scraping sound from behind me. I come up too quickly and hit my head on the edge of the table.

"Fuck!"

The scraping has become more insistent, and it's coming from the area over the sink. Six months ago, we had a rat problem over at the east side of the estate. They had eaten their way through a section of concrete from the sewers. The only reason they were able to do that was because the concrete was cast without iron mesh. I came up with the bright idea of using a drain camera to find the rats' access point, then installed a rat flap from the main sewage pipe. Giving them exit from the estate but no entrance.

I got a pat on the shoulder for that and an M&S gift voucher.

This was not rats.

I'm questioning what my eyes are looking at. I know I banged my head, but I didn't hit it that hard.

But there it is in front of me.

I can see into the wall over the sink. I know what it should look like. White tiles and a painted wall. But it's transparent enough that I can see a blurry kaleidoscopic light show erupting inside. At first, I think this is some sort of ultra-fashionable appliance you would install in your kitchen to give it some excitement. This is not Chelsea; this is Acton. Residents have more pressing life choices than to beautify their kitchens like a millionaire baller. I have a horrible feeling these special effects aren't special or effects. This is the weird and frightening smashing into my reality like a train collision again. It's becoming a habit I do not appreciate.

I step back and can feel the weight of the metal bar in my hand pressing on my fingers. I can't pry my eyes away from the throbbing colors that at first made no sense to me, but slowly I begin to see something that makes my blood chill. Each pulse of colorful light reveals what looked like eight large worm-like creatures the length of my forearm, happily moving around, eating their way through the concrete and giving off some kind of radiation that is bestowing me with X-ray vision.

"What the hell?"

I'm standing in a resident's kitchen, lit up from the reflected light like I'm in those old discotheque's, and I'm watching these things going about their business in the wall. I must've been hyperventilating because my head feels light. What comes next surprises me. I'm assailed by a clarity of thinking that makes my breath hitch. I have no idea where it came from or why I'm about to do it, but it feels right.

I reach for a pot on the draining board and fill it with cold water. I step back and fling it on the wall. The reaction is immediate. There is a crackle like a short circuit. The microwave switches itself on. The lights overhead flicker, then the fluorescent tube above me explodes into a shower of glass and white powder. I don't take my eyes off the wall. I can't.

The worms go crazy for a moment, throwing off even more light energy into the kitchen like a muted firework display in the cramped enclosure. Then the luminescence begins flickering, and the languid crawling pace they had exhibited earlier is replaced with a herky-jerky scuttle away from the damp area. There is a screech that grates my nerves, making me cringe. It's the sound of distress from the things in the wall, and it makes the hairs at the back of my neck stand on end, making sure my sleep tonight won't be a peaceful one.

My breathing is labored like I've just run a mile, and I'm trembling. The transparent wall is opaque again. The scratching sound has disappeared, and I'm standing in the chaos, knowing this time that what just happened was real.

11.

"What have we got here then?" Jerod Weiss said, shaking his head and narrowing his eyes at the state of his work in progress. He looked at the damage to the herbaceous plants and wondered if it had been used for target practice. This kind of needless vandalism made him angry.

As the landscape gardener, he was the one who made sure Spikeway Housing won the Estate Garden of the year for four years running. Jerod was an independent contractor for five housing estates. His favorite project had always been Columbia Housing Estate, even though they had never won any awards for his work.

Accolades were good, but it was more than that. The tenants had always respected his creativity in the gardens, and sometimes even done some weeding work in his absence. Now that was pleasurable work.

Spikeway, on the other hand, required more attention. Over the last few days, it seemed they needed more than he could give. Spikeway was like his base of operation, and that came about due to his relationship with the management. Spikeway Housing was so easy to work with that he found himself more often than not looking after the plants in the park or the three satellite gardens scattered around the estate. He'd been here for four years and made solid friendships with the estate team of Clayton and Steven, but he'd never seen anything like this kind of damage over one night before.

The plant beds he had set almost two weeks ago had been utterly destroyed by what he could only describe as several corkscrew holes forming deep into the ground. What was more maddening was he couldn't explain what he was looking at. All the plants had been plucked out meticulously, leaving behind this spiral impression in the mud like a wine enthusiast had got to them. Most people would pass the damage and think it was a part of his process.

It did look neat.

Neat or not, Jerod had nothing to do with this. Something else was bothering him too. To be as effective as he was in the art of landscape gardening, you had to be able to recognize the magic in detail. And although this was blatant vandalism, his eye for detail told him there was something odd about the layout of the plants. Jerod thought he should call Clayton and get him over here but decided to have another look before talking to anyone.

He lowered himself onto his hands and knees, smelling the soil and the grass, reminding himself why he loved this job so much. He stooped in the center of what was twelve holes. Whatever had tunneled into the soil through the grass had neatly replaced the turf over it once it was done. This wasn't something a vandal would do. Jerod wondered if OCD hooligans were a thing. Gently, he took the grassy top off one of the holes and pushed his arm into it. The hole accommodated him, but its length seemed to go on. The inside was smooth, like glass or porcelain - the kind of feeling you would expect if a massive heat source had shot into the earth.

Jerod wasn't one for funny feelings, but how else could he explain the tingling at the base of his spine? Out of habit and thoroughness, he checked the plants that circled the holes. There were a few shrubs, but it was mainly grass and something else tangled into it. He had been so focused on the holes, he hadn't noticed a running plant that wound its way around the others like it needed everyone's attention. Jerod didn't recognize what it was and came over to examine it.

"Strange."

Whatever it was, it had a dark green hue, scaly and elongated with a few mottled white flowers, with pink blotches like bruises on white skin. The plant seemed to be modifying its hue to match its surrounding, similar to a camouflage trait. Jerod pushed his nose closer to this strange runner. It obviously didn't like the attention as it tightened its grip on the branches surrounding it, much like a snake would.

"Whoa!"

That reaction took him by surprise, and so did what came next. A lone flower on the runner plant turned to face him, a hissing sound coming through its leaves and stems. Jerrod jerked back, falling on his arse. The flower that was not a flower lunged at him again. A hissing rattling sound issued from its stamen, if that's what it was because it looked more reptilian than plant, exhibiting a sinewy movement as if it was sensing the environment, like the tongue of a snake. It was also mimicking Jerod's retreat, like something a cobra would do.

He was transfixed at a safe distance, watching in amazement, his head feeling light from the rush of fear and surprise. That disappeared quickly, and the cold light of reality stubbornly remained.

What had he discovered?

The plant thing, happy it had protected its environment, retreated into the shrub, the surrounding greenery seemed to get brighter as it blended in perfectly with its background. Jerod took a deep breath and was just about to push himself up to standing when he heard the spitting sounds and felt the needle pricks in his neck and cheeks. He immediately felt a rush of warmth, then a slow creep of cold and sudden immobilization. His body stiffened, every muscle locked rigid. He hit the soft turf like a plank of wood.

Jerod could breathe and could see, but that was as far as his nervous system allowed. He was trapped in his own body. He screamed and screamed again, but it was all in his head.

12.

Ylak was alone in the ladies' locker room of the community center. It was a big room with a long bench in the middle and lockers surrounding it. She imagined it wasn't used much by the females of the species because dust particulates were everywhere. Being in here was conforming to what a young Earth woman would do. She didn't have much to store anyway except for a jacket and handbag, but it felt sufficient; this was acceptable behavior.

The replicated university jumpsuit was good enough to protect her clothes. A laptop computer of the brand Apple had been augmented for her purposes and was in a backpack with the rest of the research tools which she always had with her. She sat on the bench and tied her boots, still getting used to her two feet, then checked the multipurpose watch on her hand.

She sighed.

There was not much time to do this and being handicapped by the rules of engagement when working within the confines of inferior civilizations made the job so much more difficult. She may not look it in her human form as Nikki, but as Ylak Marr, she was taught how to adapt in hostile environments and preferred when the challenges came directly with teeth and claw. It was about time she used some of her more subtle training.

Ylak thought about it, then stood up and headed towards the entrance of the community center. The humans considered this beautiful weather, but Ylak almost didn't notice. Swirling around in her head was her plan of action. She may even talk to Clayton and try to find out some more of what he knew. He was an interesting specimen. She just needed to approach it carefully. Ylak walked down the path to the main road and took a shorter route across the small roundabout towards the park. Ylak knew the Omni-Seed had crash-landed here and knew it had begun experimenting with altering the genetics of the lower species.

From her experience and research on Sigma Minor, the Omni-Seed would actively destroy any civilization and promote the growth of lower lifeforms. It seemed to be an evolutionary imperative that subdued any species with a hope of establishing complex societies and technology. It had hidden itself masterfully amongst the human dwellings, and Ylak had an inkling the Omni-Seed's homeworld would be more forgiving. She pushed the creaky gate open and started heading up the path.

The Park had been broken up into grids of equal areas, and each grid was analyzed with the advanced technology at her disposal. Half of the park was already done. The other half she was hoping to complete analyzing today. She made her way over to the area she had left yesterday evening. Ylak came up to the shrubs that grew on the fringes of the park. She unslung her shoulder bag and let it fall to the grass. A soft murmuring made her stop and look around.

Ylak checked to see if anyone was watching her. She ran her hand over the fleshy sound collecting appendage, and like a magic trick, her human ear shimmered then disappeared. Replacing it was a mound of green speckled flesh that vibrated like a drum skin. She snapped her head around and pinpointed the origin of the sound. Something ahead of her was struggling to breathe or trying to get someone's attention. Ylak sprinted over to another set of shrubs and shifted briefly from her human eyesight to the multi-spectral sensors she was born with. It came into clarity as she stared straight at it.

The optical illusion was effective.

The groundsman was wrapped in a light-refracting cocoon excreted by what could only be a Kirillian spider. This deadly evolutionary tag team worked seamlessly to bring down some of the largest animal life in the wetlands. The plant would incapacitate its prey, the spider would camouflage then digest its food, and both would share its nutrients. Except this was not Torian 5, this was Earth, and over three days, the Omni-Seed had managed to transmute indigenous lifeforms to new species.

Ylak had a sinking feeling in an unfamiliar gut, her focus shifting to survival as the consequences of what she was looking at dawned on her. Snapping out of her chaos thinking, she had a life to save. Quickly, Ylak reached into her bag and slipped her awkward five fingers into a medi-glove. Her fingertips glowed red, and with a sweeping motion of her hands, she began melting away the cocoon revealing the man inside. In moments, she was hard at work saving the alien's life and wondering if she would be called on to do the same for the whole planet.

13.

I watch the ambulance disappear around the corner with Jerod in the back. I feel like I'm standing on the slopes of a strange volcano that had suddenly appeared in my backyard. I know it will erupt soon but don't know when. The tremors are everywhere, all the telltale signs it will be bad, but I just can't string together a sensible, rational explanation for what is going on.

That makes me nervous.

"I should have gone with him," I say.

"But you couldn't, man," Steven says, trying to make me see sense. "Let's get the paperwork done, and we can go visit him after work."

I nod, knowing he is right, and turn to Nikki who stands just behind us looking on, her stare kind of vacant for a moment. She snaps back to the present when she realizes she is the center of attention.

"If you hadn't been there," I say, "this would have turned out so much worse. Thanks."

"It was the least I could do. I'm just lucky to have come out when I did. Did you know that Jerod was violently allergic to bee stings?"

I think about it for a moment, but it's something that never came up in our many conversations.

"I didn't have a clue," I admit. "What makes you think it was bees anyway?"

Nikki smiles.

"The offending culprit died on his arm after stinging him. When you do a lot of fieldwork like me, you pick up a few survival skills as you go."

Steven has been quiet while we talked. I can tell he is impressed by Nikki's skills.

"How's your investigation coming along then?" Steven asks. "The rats and stuff."

"Oh yes," she hesitates, then catches on to what Steven is asking. "It's coming along. I have discovered a few mutations and their breeding habits."

I'm interested in her work, having just qualified for my pest control certification, but I've not had an opportunity to engage with her. And yet, I feel she can help me with my problems. How do I broach the question without sounding weird or crazy? Something strange and dangerous was happening on the estate, and I don't think I can handle it alone. I'm gonna have to trust somebody. I hope to ignite her enthusiasm with a leading question. I'm hoping she's less of a chicken shit than I am and expresses her concerns.

"Have you noticed anything strange?" I ask. From the corner of my eye, I see Steven looking at me curiously. I know what's going through his head. I've asked him the same question before, and he tried to figure out what I was smoking. I never let on, and here it was again. Steven was either getting concerned with my secrecy or pissed off.

Nikki doesn't look surprised by the question at all. It's almost as if she was expecting something unusual, the way she hangs on to her shoulder bag as she watches me speak. I'm not that interesting. I can't help but think the question excited her.

She hesitates.

"It's been an uneventful day, actually. Outside of some rats with an extra toe, it's been quiet. I wouldn't call that strange, would you?"

Steven laughs.

"Should we be worried?" he asks.

"It happens naturally in all species," Nikki says. "You should be fine."

"So, you saw nothing that surprised you?" I press.

"Why do you ask?"

"I've seen some peculiar vermin activity. Just thought you may have experienced it too." I finesse the truth.

"Nothing out of the ordinary," Nikki says. "So far, I have been concentrating in one area. There is another sector I need to investigate." She pauses to think about it. "It may involve some night work, and who knows, I may discover something strange there." Her eyes light up.

"You really love your work, don't you?" I ask. "Working a night shift is above and beyond the call of duty. You're either on a tight deadline or there's overtime?" I grin.

Nikki looks at me blankly with those beautiful brown eyes. I can almost see her missing the point as it flies over her head. She does that sometimes, and in those instances, it's like she's 'processing'.

Yes, it is becoming a thing.

She is back with me.

"Just eager. And talking about being eager, I need to get back to work."

"Of course, of course. I just meant to say thanks again." I say.

"And again," Nikki smiles, "I'm glad I could help."

"We'll leave you to it then," Steven nods.

I smile at her as I walk away with work-shy Steven in tow. Nikki turns back to her bag which is still on the grass and adds as an afterthought, "If I find anything strange, I'll be sure to let you know first."

I'm not sure if she is being serious or not, but that sounded like an invitation.

14.

I step out of the Iron Planet gym, tingling from a sauna I had subjected myself to and hoping to shake the morose vibe following me around like a bad smell. After all that, the despondent fog drifts outside with me. My workout was suffering too. It just didn't feel the same today, and I justify it by saying I have a lot on my mind. I repeat the words to myself.

I'll feel better at work today.

I'll feel better at work today.

My mantra doesn't work.

Okay, it is good being absorbed in something I love doing, and seeing Nikki around is a bonus. But what if the thing I love is causing me to question everything I understood about the world I inhabit?

I shrug.

"You alright, mate?" I stop and turned to face the tall bearded handsome features of Sebastian. He is standing outside the gym with arms folded and a look of concern on his face. If I ever develop the discipline to build proper muscle, I want to look like him. His definition is crazy but not freakish. I'd cast him for a role as Hercules without batting an eyelid. The makeup team would have to remove the tattoos on his neck, arms, chest, and legs, and then work on his South African accent, but other than that, he'd make a perfect Roman demi-God.

He smiles at me.

"Talking to yourself again," he teases.

"Yeah," I raise my eyebrows. "Madness or genius. You choose."

I notice Sebastian's posture shift from his initial welcome to a more severe shuffle. I get on really well with him and his partner. They've invited me in many times for lunch and, except for their love of everything Kylie Minogue, they were ideal residents.

"How's it going?" I ask again.

Sebastian sighs and creases his lips.

"I know you're not on the clock yet, but Tom and I are worried…" He corrects himself. "We are concerned about Mr. Faulkner, our neighbor."

The mental picture of the odd married couple of Tom with his button-down shirt and Sebastian with his tats makes me smile.

"Faulkner?" The name rings a bell, but the memory of him doesn't coalesce into a mental image until Sebastian helps my recollection.

"He drives trains and owns that silver Mercedes AMG. The one my other half gets all hot and bothered over when he sees it drive by."

"I know the brother," I confirm with an air of excitement. His ride is dope. "He loves that car," I say.

"And that's one of the reasons why we're concerned," Sebastian says. "I haven't seen him, he's not answering his door, and neither has he driven his car in the past twenty-four hours."

He slips one of his veined hands into the pocket of his grey tracksuit bottoms out of habit or nervousness. His thighs are Olympian. "He's not answering his phone either."

You hear stories about the diminishing community spirit of Londoners. People dead in their homes four weeks before they're found. A society much too busy surviving to be their neighbor's keeper is simply not true. I'm staring at one of the many thousands of exceptions. I think about Sebastian's concerns and understand.

"Should I call the police?" Sebastian asks.

I lower my head to think about it.

"No," I say, finally coming up for air. "Let me look around first."

I'm suddenly struck by my privileged position. Me, a youngster in comparison to the residents I look after. They trust my opinion and listen to what I have to say. My forehead tingles at the thought of it. I try not to take it lightly.

"Tell you what, I start work in two hours. What if I meet you at home, and we can look into it together?"

Sebastian nods, his broad shoulders lowering slightly as he unconsciously shrugs off a wave of tension.

"You guys are good neighbors," I say.

"What other kind is there?"

I smile at him.

"I'll meet you in two," I turn to go but stop and look back at the big man. "It's gonna be fine."

I need to get into competitive poker because it isn't going to be all right. I can feel it.

Almost three hours later, I stand beside Tom and Sebastian, staring intently at the silver Mercedes AMG. I had just entered Mr. Faulkner's apartment using the locksmith services of Stewie, our go-to guy for legal breaking and entering. The apartment was empty, and just as Sebastian and Tom had thought, it seemed Mr. Faulkner hadn't been there for a while. His kitchen was clean and orderly. The mail was still stuffed in the mail flap and some on the mat. All this time, I was trying to process everything I was seeing. That was until we left the flat and walked down to the parking area to his car.

Looking down from his apartment, the car was in a perfect line of sight. There was something about its sexy curves and futuristic styling that gave me the chills. And not in a good way either. I'm sure that's not how I should have felt as I walked towards it. I just couldn't shake the feeling that somehow the car held the answers to this mystery. Eventually, I ambled up to the bumper without a plan, with a kind of tunnel vision, vaguely aware the two residents were behind me.

I'm staring at the Mercedes, standing right in front of it, my knees touching the bumper, and my image appears on the dust-streaked windshield. The car's interior looks as clean and orderly as his flat. I may seem to know what I'm doing, and if I'm giving that impression, then I'm better than I give myself credit for. If I'm honest, Clayton French is being led by gut instinct that I never knew I had.

I press my finger down on the hood, and it gives me some play. A Mercedes engineer would not be happy with that. I rub my finger along the gap between the hood and the grill. Something is stuck between it. I feel around for the latch, release it and lever the hood upwards. I nearly drop it back in place and walk away. Thought and action did not work in unison, and I stand there, arms trembling. I blink once, then again, as if to confirm what my eyes are telling me. Something is very, very wrong.

The engine compartment is lacking an engine. I'm not saying the engine was no good; what I'm saying is there is no engine at all, just a gaping hole. It hasn't been ripped out; there is no damage to the surrounding engine compartment, no scratches, no dents. Rubber conduits, plastic sheath wires, and pipes hang down like anemones growing from the coral reef of a metal interior. The engine might as well have melted away, leaving no residue. Except for the plastic remnants that are not absorbed but strewn on the ground, there is nothing above that says an engine has ever been bolted into place here except…

I lean over and lower my head. Amongst the discarded plastic engine parts on the oil-stained ground, something peeks up from the mound.

I close the hood.

I crouch in front of the car and look under the carriage on all fours. A squeaky sound of surprise squeezes from my throat as I quickly stand up and back away, turning to Sebastian.

"Can you ring his phone again?" I ask him.

Wordlessly, Tom's fingers dance over his smartphone screen. With a couple seconds delay, there is a ring coming from under the car.

My blood chills.

Tom slaps a trembling hand to his mouth, and Sebastien hugs him.

I find myself dropping my head, breathing harder than I should, and my eyes become prickly as if they are readying for tears. Not the reaction I expected, but things are suddenly getting real. I look around and I see Nikki walking towards me from the lawn surrounding the block of flats. I'm trying to read her expression as she hurries my way, and at the same time, I hope she can't interpret my look of despair. I wipe my eyes, and I feel hot and dazed.

"All good?" I ask as if anything about this situation would ever be good again. Nikki ignores me and stoops, taking out a handheld device which she points inches from the ground. She then beckons me over.

"Look," she says.

I come up beside her and bend down to see the VDU screen. It takes me a moment to get used to as it looks like multiple small screens grouped together, but my eyes adjust. It looks like microscopic images at high modification.

"What am I looking at?" I ask.

"Tracks," she says. "Or, to be more specific,

trails."

I look away from Nikki's impressive piece of kit and look at the silvery band about three feet wide and inordinate length that snake from under the Mercedes, across the footpath, and into the park.

"How come I can see that trail now?" The trail that had been invisible to me moments ago has suddenly appeared like invisible ink after looking through her device.

I turn to Nikki.

"What's that?" I point to the handheld gizmo attached to her belt. Her eyes look up as she processes my question.

"Something like a portable mass spectrometer with an organic modifier."

"That sounds expensive," I say. And without waiting for an answer, I ask. "It enhanced my eyesight, didn't it?"

Nikki looks at me and says nothing.

"I bet you know what made those trails?"

Nikki shrugs.

"I'm just as...mystified as you, Clayton. When I discovered it, I followed it here."

Why am I not surprised by her answer? Right place at the right time. She has a knack for that.

"I did say if I find anything strange, I'd let you know. Well, this is strange."

She thinks about what she is about to say. Or is it one of the moments of processing?

"These trails look like something left behind by a gastropod fifteen times the size of a normal Earth snail." She hesitates, then refocuses. "And we both know that is not possible, right?"

Is that a question of fact or a statement of uncertainty? I ponder her words in the confines of my own head.

Earth snails.

Her device and now my mind are latching onto those two words for analysis.

Earth snails.

Who would say that?

I feel Sebastian's presence before I see him.

"What's going on, Clayton?" the big man asks, looking at me, then Nikki.

"I really don't know what to think." I'm genuinely struggling, but I have to do something. I sigh.

"From what we've seen, it's not looking good. Let's not waste any more time; let's call in the Old Bill."

I leave the car scene with my nerves jangling, and a headache that made me feel like tiny fragments of my skull are dislodging.

Why do I have the stomach-churning feeling that this is only the beginning?

15.

Be careful what you wish for. I'm beginning to understand how true Aesop's saying was. I wanted an opportunity to prove my worth.

Well, Clayton, my son, I've been given that opportunity in spades over the last four days.

I'm hurrying over to Block D because I have just received a weird call from Mr. Jenkins.

What now?

I'm still weak in the knees from what I've just experienced. The thought did cross my mind to cut my day short while I was ahead. Feeling scared was one thing, shirking on my responsibilities was another. All the way over, I'm praying he's okay. Mr. J is a delivery driver and resident. The man loves what he does with an almost romantic zeal. The stories he would tell you about the loads he's taken and had the pleasure and sometimes displeasure of transporting to different parts of the city was enthralling.

He is a natural storyteller. Thursday was his rejuvenation day, as he chose to call it. Time to absorb what he had learned in the week. That was the kind of man he was. Mindfulness wasn't just a buzzword for him; it was a way of life. Hearing panic in his voice is unusual. He is the calmest person I knew. When I get to Number 45, the door is partially open, and my mind flashes back to Maggie and the luminescent worms in her wall. My heart is pounding and not just from the run. I knock once and call out.

"Mr. J," I push it open without waiting for a reply. I'm relieved to see Mr. J standing in the middle of his small living room in his grey underpants and a crisp white wife-beater vest.

"Can you feel it?" he asks me, and I just look at him, confused at the question.

"You had me worried. Are you okay?"

"Something is wrong, Clayton," he says slowly,

his eyes looking frantic and me having no idea what is going on.

"How so?" I ask. I'm starting to wonder if he is suffering from a mental episode, not that I would know what one of those looked like.

"Something is disturbing the peace; the balance of the estate is all wrong."

Didn't Percy say something like that?

"Has that snot-nosed git from Number 15 been messing with you again?" I ask, not expecting Mr. J to smile.

"Have you ever woken up and just felt that while you slept, something around you, everything around you has subtly changed?"

I kinda knew what he was talking about. I usually felt that way the day after a pub crawl with Steven.

I nod, and the whole building vibrates with such violence, I'm knocked to my knees.

Motes of dust bellow from the cracks and seams.

"Do you feel it now?" Mr. J nods in a way that requires me to nod too.

"I feel it, I feel it!" I say, assessing escape routes and protection points.

I've never experienced an earthquake in my life. I've seen films and documentaries and heard first-hand accounts of the terror. And for some reason, I remember they recommend you hit the ground and take cover under sturdy furniture. It made sense. But I'm Clayton French, goddamit, the hero. Experts with years of experience are telling me what to do, and I simply ignore them.

I grab Mr. J and start making my way through the front door as another tremor ripples through the building. Once I get onto the landing, I start knocking on Mr. J's neighbors' doors as I go, just in case anyone is hurt. It's more of a gesture because I can't wait and see. We walk briskly to the short flight of stairs, taking them three at a time so we can get to open space as quickly as possible. Mr. J is keeping up with me, and as I burst out into the open air, he is about ten steps behind me in his boxers and wife-beaters. I've forgotten he didn't have time to change. It seems to be a thing as about a dozen people in varying degrees of undress huddle in a group, looking suspiciously at the building. I start hearing my name as the tenants recognize me.

"Is everybody okay?" I ask.

"What just happened?" somebody asks me.

"Earthquake," Tom from Number 15, or was it 17, says.

Mrs. Sharpe laughs.

"Earthquake? We don't get earthquakes in West London."

And I have to agree, it wasn't a seismic event at all. I'm beginning to think it's the building. While the tenants speak amongst themselves, I amble back over to the flats, my head still and steady, but I have a theory. I stand at the main entrance and appraise the building. It's glaringly obvious when you pay attention.

The entire block is askew.

One corner of the building has sunk into the ground by maybe a foot or more. For some reason, the foundations weakened, and the building subsided, leaving ugly looking massive fissure running up the side of the building like a lightning bolt. My head is getting clearer, and I'm making connections that earlier in the panic I couldn't. I reach for my mobile and call emergency services and then, reluctantly, my bosses.

16.

Ylak had to admit she enjoyed working at night on this planet. Walking on two legs was a problem, but Uncle's human consciousness algorithm allowed her to adapt quickly. After all, that is what her species had been bred to do. Some were better than others, but she was the best amongst her people. She had been chosen from more than a hundred other siblings, elevating her brood to the history trees, forever remembered in the bark and esteemed by generations.

Earth was different from her homeworld of Magnox Prime, but at night, if she focused inwards there were echoes of home here. It was relaxing, with all its little wars raging, ecological challenges, financial disparities and a whole host of growing pains a fledgling civilisation must experience. For her, Earth's potential greatness could be sensed in the still of night when human minds synchronised in sleep and their higher consciousness revealed itself. Faced with that dazzling distraction she had to remember to remain vigilant. There was a time limit to her efforts, and the stakes were high not just for herself but for an entire planet. This was her doing, choices she made against Uncle's cold logic. The thinking that got her here could not get her out of it. Ylak would avail herself of the beauty of the planet when she finished her job.

At this moment, she reminded herself of what she had done so far. Ylak had logged ten minor zombie species that the Omni-Seed had transformed. Wherever the Omni-Seed was garrisoned, Ylak presumed it had started transforming whatever creatures its hyper senses discovered in its neighborhood. From their last encounter, the seed-mind had control over an area of 27 Krogs-1 square. What she couldn't understand was why it had chosen this nest of humans.

One thing was clear, the Omni-Seed had obviously learned from its last encounter on jungle planet Sigma Minor. Tracking it had proven difficult, almost impossible before. What complicated matters even more was the earth minerals reacting with her equipment. Her effectiveness was compromised by the consideration of human casualties, and what was already complicated became infuriating.

Four possible locations of the seed-mind had come back negative. She had five drones on twenty-four-hour rotation, and still, she was unable to detect irregular fluctuations in power outputs. The Omni-Seed must need vast amounts of energy to manipulate and force evolution in a species the way it does, but Uncle hadn't been able to work out how.

Ylak looked at the flickering blue-hued hologram that projected an image of a hundred meters underground on the scanner unit she rested on the grass. The four probes transmitting the information back to the receiver unit bored straight down into the grid system she set up. It seemed to be picking up emanations from the sewage pipes deep in the ground. If she had to guess, this was another phantom signal.

How it was able to do that, Ylak couldn't say, but

it had learned some new tricks since it landed on Earth or while she was in cryo-sleep. Ylak had to adapt quickly, or all this would end badly for planet Earth, one human nest at a time. Trying to resolve this and keep the sanctity of the planet to define its own destiny was not just difficult but could prove to be impossible. This investigation had been ramped up from extraction to elimination.

Ylak did not have the luxury of time to contain the threat. This operation would require some kind of intervention from the indigenous people. That decision the System Alliance would never forgive if they found out. Clayton and Steven would be the support she needed. She had to find a way not just to tell them but to include them in this search. In the meantime, as well as formulating a plan of action to find the seed, she must consider how she would approach them.

She would start with Clayton. For some reason, her simulated human heart was beating a little faster when she thought of him.

17.

Now, I know what being overwhelmed feels like. I've been helping the Spikeway Housing Association in collaboration with the Council to rehouse residents affected by the building's subsidence. It's a tedious job, but I know my off and on help is appreciated. I still have my duties to attend to and my hair-brain theories to prove. Through it all, my gut is constantly tight, my limbs feel weak with nervous tremors, and I'm hyper-vigilant. This is unfamiliar territory, but I will soldier through it. What choice do I have?

Complaints from residents aren't my favorite thing to handle, but it's a good distraction from the craziness surrounding me. And Mr. Rutherford will not let me forget it. The owner of Flat 57 is an older gentleman, annoyingly persistent but harmless, who wants something done about a noise nuisance on the penthouse level. The residents call the top floor of Fenchurch House the IceCap. The name came about partially because the penthouse was painted snow-white, but if you spoke to the younger, more street residents, they'll tell you another more pertinent reason for its nickname.

It's six stories up to the top, and it's one of the only five residences owned by a private individual. Spikeway Housing controls the rest and, usually, the arrangement works well. The owners have a nine-hundred-year lease and pay ground rent to help with the upkeep of the surrounding infrastructure. Four of the owners are quite laid back, but owner number five, the deed holder of the IceCap, imagines this is his own high-rise fiefdom. I'd heard about his snide remarks, his passive-aggressive attitude, and his little coke habit. I relish the idea of 'setting deh bwoy straight', as my dad would say.

Greg Simon or DJ Greggo was a name on the UK

DJ circuit. He was a bit of a dick who made his next-in-line superstar status go to his peroxide blonde head. My first clash with him had been when he just bought the property nearly two years ago. DJ Greggo drove a Porsche 911 and was demanding two car spaces for his prize possession. When he was denied, he tried to bully other residents, especially Miss Huxley, who reminded me of my grandmother, into giving him what he wanted. It didn't go his way, and ever since, we've had a war of words when our paths crossed. It never developed into anything more than that, although if I didn't match his physicality - we both love the gym - he may have taken steps.

Catching my breath and composing myself, I press the buzzer to a white door that looks like it had been buffed and shined to an inch of its life. I can see my reflection on its surface as I step back to wait. Even where I'm standing, I can barely feel the vibration of the music through the door. I wonder what his audio setup is like and quickly dismiss the thought. The door rattles from the inside, and I think it's the music buffeting the interior, but it turns out to be latches being pulled and the chain being released.

The door swings open; no looking through the peephole for him, or he had already established I was harmless. Out floods a sweet floral scent and dancehall music. The botanical aroma is lush, carried by a damp heat like he has left the heating on at the highest setting. The music is excellent too. No watered-down European appropriated garbage. This is the real McCoy from Jamaica. I'm trying my damnedest not to warm to him, but he is making it difficult. I'm impressed.

He looks statuesque, tanned, and barefooted in gym shorts and a tight-fitting vest over a muscled chest and abs. A pair of expensive-looking cans are slung around his neck. He eyes me up and down, a sneer forming on his lips when he recognizes who I was.

"What can I do you for?" he asks lazily.

I step back, and it's my turn to look him up and down. The last time we had words, he was trying to intimidate me by stepping into my personal space.

It didn't work then and may not work now.

I clear my throat and step up to him.

"One of the residents reported a disturbance a few nights ago, coming from your apartment."

DJ Greggo sighs then asked, "What kind of disturbance?"

"Sounds," I say, only then realizing how vague that is. "Not music but repeating brain-numbing sounds, I was told. It went on for ages, your neighbors said."

"It was that busy body snitch Mr. Rutherford, wasn't it?"

I shrug, not agreeing or disagreeing. The DJ doesn't pause to hear if I have an opinion.

"Did you hear the music from outside my door?"

Thinking about it now, I didn't.

It dawns on me.

"Your apartment's soundproof," I say.

An ugly smile appears on his face.

"Yeah," the DJ says. "So that lying toe-rag has just wasted your time."

I know Mr. Rutherford well. He may be a bit overbearing, but a liar he isn't, and neither is Mrs. Logan. Something else must have gone on that night with everything else that I couldn't explain. I wasn't letting DJ Greggo off the hook so easily, not just yet.

"Okay, it wasn't you, but you must have heard something." A movement behind him catches my eye.

My focus shifts from his face and into the space behind him. The figure that made me look is naked, dark-skinned, curvaceous, and giggling as she streaks behind the DJ and holds him. He doesn't skip a beat.

"Listen, Mr. Groundsman, I heard nothing; I saw nothing. I had my hands full," he grins lecherously, snaking his hands behind his back, grabbing a handful of arse and inciting more squeals from the chick behind him.

"Okay," I say, biting my lip. "Sorry to bother you."

DJ Greggo looks at me carefully and nods. The air from inside his apartment is so sweet, I want to step through. But before I come to my senses, the door is swinging shut, and I hear the DJ say, "Anytime, groundsman, anytime."

18.

I'm sitting on my mom's sofa in her quaint Caribbean-themed front room. She protects her pristine décor with a vengeance and hates me being in there, but I have a guest. And guests are sacrosanct. I plump up one of her cushions self-consciously. I don't know what else to do. Maybe because it's seven-thirty in the morning and I still have sleep in my eyes, and I'm dressed in England shorts and a Reggae Boyz T-shirt. My look of shock and bewilderment didn't come about because of my choice of sleepwear. No, the cause of my befuddlement is some existential shit that nobody should be subjected to this early in the morning before coffee.

Nikki is an alien.

Let that sink in.

She's standing there looking all cute in her university jumpsuit, and I'm repeating to myself that this is not funny. I'm about to ask her for the fifth time what she is talking about. I can take a wind up as good, if not better than the next man. I'm also good at realizing when the joke is over and the punchline exhausted, especially with evidence. She hands me a multi-sided object that I think is a tetrahedron. Mr. Harris, my maths teacher, would be disappointed I'd forgotten. It's cool to the touch and tingling.

"Place it on the floor," she says to me.

Which I do.

She smiles. Who wouldn't get a laugh out of a grown man stumbling around at the announcement that we are not alone in the universe? Nikki looks directly at the object and speaks. Well, actually, it feels like a command and is issued not from her mouth but all over her body. A set of vibrations that is so bizarre and unfamiliar, I hear a part of it in my ears and a sharp resonance at the back of my head. I wince.

"What the fuck was that?" I ask, massaging my

temple.

"My language," Nikki says, this time words and sounds coming from her mouth. "Not designed for the human ear. Want to hear some more?"

She is enjoying this a bit too much.

"No, thank you," I decline, my attention diverted to the tetrahedron in the middle of the room that has just come alive. Streams of light are shooting out from its surface. The multicolored beams move faster than my eyes can follow, almost stitching a pattern in the air above, creating an optical tapestry that becomes an ultra-high-definition image of what looks like an alien egg.

It makes my skin crawl.

"Let me introduce you to the Omni-Seed," Nikki says.

It's ovoid in shape, about three times the size of a football, its surface is cancerous, a patchwork of lizard-like skin and pulsing pustules.

I get up from my seat and run my fingers through the image and watch it shimmer and then reassemble into a perfect image again.

"What is it?" I ask.

"It's a new super organism we discovered that actively bioforms its lower species and uses them as tools to destroy civilizations and the higher species that created them. There is much we don't understand about it, but it's so specific, so intelligent, we think it didn't evolve but was created. It escaped the confines of my starship and crash-landed here."

I think about what she just said, my mind brimming with questions.

"Escape?" I ask. "How? It looks like a giant stick insect egg."

Nikki breathes heavily. I'm wondering if she's holding back on explaining the more esoteric science our world has no idea about.

"Not only is the Omni-Seed strategically brilliant, but it can also psionically transform the genetic makeup of organisms from a distance. It locates and sculpts them to its specifications by means we are still studying, so they become the perfect soldiers in its war against progress. It uses these same creatures to transport and hide it."

"Damn. I was impressed with cockroaches – a resilient Earth insect," I clarify.

Nikki's eyelids flutter as she processes then nods.

"Now they are true survivors, maybe not an apocalypse but evolutionary engineered to keep coming. I know, those buggers are hard to exterminate – I've had a few on the estate, but they're dumb. This Omni-Seed is another level smart."

"Completely," Nikki agrees with me.

"You know what it's doing, don't you?" I say as the thought comes to me.

"Inform me." Nikki's eyes brighten.

"It's testing the waters. It's experimenting with Earth animals, perfecting its skill, getting used to our genetics and seeing how its transformations are doing." I nod my head as if I'm agreeing with myself. "It started small and now it's getting more ambitious. That's what I'd do."

Nikki looks at me strangely, then nods.

"This is a new environment for the Omni-Seed and it's…finding its feet. But we can't allow it to get comfortable. That could be disastrous."

My mind is racing a mile a minute.

"How did you get to our Solar System?" I ask sheepishly.

"A shifting network of what you call Einstein – Rosenberg bridges that connect the furthest of galaxies."

A wormhole. My mouth falls open, but before I can continue my line of enquiry, Nikki loses her cool.

"Do you believe me?" she snaps.

I nod my head vigorously, and it feels like any moment, my astral self could detach from my physical body. I am not a weed smoker, but the few times I had puffed on a spliff, I had a similar out-of-body experience, one of the reasons I stay away from the stuff. This is different and the same all at once. Can you believe I fancy a bonafide extraterrestrial?

"Why did you choose to tell me," I ask, my words slow and deliberate like Nikki - if that is her real name - doesn't understand English.

"I think we're both interested in the same thing."

Thinking is difficult, and one part of my mind is expecting me to wake up, but the situation remains stubbornly real. I look to the door leading into the room where I'm sat and wonder how I will explain the crazy hologram to my mother if she steps through the door. I almost wish she would. I need something, anything to shatter this surreal drama unfolding in my sitting room. In a minute, my mind catches up to Nikki's conversation.

"What thing is that?" I dumbly ask.

She sighs.

"Every strange occurrence that has happened over the last week. That thing."

It starts to all make sense to me in an avalanche of crystal clarity. Nikki's sudden appearance investigating rats, her cool tech, the strange creatures, the unexplained building subsidence, fires and disappearances, cats and dogs vanishing, and the meteor shower.

"That," Nikki points to the floating image, "is the cause of your worries. And if I don't capture and neutralize it, humankind as you know it will cease to exist."

My mouth falls open before I catch myself.

No pressure then, I think.

19.

Johal brought his scooter to a rolling stop and checked his satnav. The smell of pizza wafted up from his hot box, the aroma twirling around him. He regretted not memorizing the address when he was at the Pizza Delicious office, but why should he have? It was automatically sent to his navigation system which had always guided him unerringly to his destination.

Well, not tonight.

The signal to the satnav app on his phone had gone crazy, showing jagged lines of static over the map. The strange thing was that its bizarre behavior seemed to be happening only in this localized spot. The young man took off his crash helmet and looked around the estate, hoping to see someone standing outside waiting for their late-night snack. It was eerily quiet. He looked at his smartphone again, and besides the static, the screen showed no Wi-Fi and no telephone reception.

This was London; he thought this only happened in rural areas. What did they call them again, reception black spots? In his head, he threatened to change his service provider and decided to ride back out to the main road, pick up a signal, and call base for the address. He slipped his helmet back on and attempted to start his moped.

It wouldn't.

He toggled the ignition key again, but it was completely dead. A chill zig-zagged down his spine and gut, and he wasn't sure why. Johal wouldn't say this aloud, and if asked about this again, he would deny it, but the darkness of the streets began to close on him in a way he could not explain. His heart was pounding, and his breathing was elevating. He had delivered to the Spikeway Estate numerous times before, but tonight he was suddenly filled with a feeling of malice and threat.

A localized throbbing pain that started at the back of his ear then spread across the dome of his head was usually an omen of bad things to come, ever since he was a boy growing up in Delhi. He had learned to heed its insistent warnings even when it felt like a cat sharpening its claws on the soft membranes of his brain. He immediately started pushing the scooter in the direction he had come from.

Every step, he keenly watched the shifting shadows around him. He was beginning to wish he had not taken this job, wished he had feigned sickness or ignored his phone. He kept pushing his dead scooter until it almost felt as if he couldn't push it anymore. And it did feel that way. He actually couldn't push it anymore.

But it wasn't him.

He looked down at the tires, and they were trapped in a bluish viscous liquid that held fast. It had been liberally applied to the road surface from one side to the next in a wonky brushstroke like a drunk artist had tried his hand at road markings. Or, more disconcertingly, a trap set.

He had his left sneaker caught in whatever it was,

and both tires of his scooter would not budge. Just over his shoulder within the communal gardens, the shadows began to coalesce like a silent thunderstorm. It spat two globules resembling the same blue liquid on the ground from its dark, growling insides. They whistled through the air, and before Johal could respond by ducking or screaming, they both hit the hot box that contained the pizzas with a Slap! Slap! It startled him at first, but the real surprise was that the globules were tentacles stretching from the hotbox into the darkness beyond.

Johal's desperation became panic as he abandoned struggling with the scooter and tried to free himself. Whatever the thick liquid was, it adhered to his Adidas with unrelenting enthusiasm. Johal swore, reached down, fumbled with the top two sets of laces, making sure his fingers stayed away from the blue gloop, and dragged his foot out. With a kind of a hop and a run, Johal didn't look back as he heard the hotbox collapse explosively and shivered as the ravenous slurping noises coming from whatever monstrosity had taken the customer's three pepperoni and chili pizzas echoed through the night.

I've just come off the phone with Pizza Delicious, and it's not good news for us. Our usual Friday poker or dominoes game night dubbed Friday Night Live requires beers, cider, and food. The vibe is not as it should be. I just can't bring myself to relax after knowing all that is happening. I knew Steven could feel it, but it was tradition and I didn't want to be the one to ruin that. We've ordered takeaways to the Bat Cave on Friday Night Live every month for two of the three years we've worked together, but tonight that grand tradition was coming to an end.

"The estates have been blacklisted, mate," I announce.

"For fuck sake, why?" Steven moans.

I know why, and I feel guilty. I can hear his stomach grumbling from here.

"The delivery guy was attacked with our pizzas tonight, and their management has decided it's not worth the risk." I look at him and rub my fist under my lip, bristling the hairs there. "Deliveroo, UberEats, Pizza Hut, Domino's, and even Mr. Chungs won't deliver."

Steven looks up to the ceiling in dismay. It's like I have kicked him in the gut.

"Seven days since I came back from my hols," Steven says, "and this happens. Did you move in a family of muggers while I was gone?"

I sigh deeply and lower my head.

There and then, I decide I have to come clean and tell him the truth.

"You like Nikki, don't you?" I ask him.

He looks at me, puzzled.

"Yeah..." Steven hesitates.

"Well…"

20.

The day after I dashed cold water all over Steven's Friday Night Live and revealed an alien invasion on his doorstep, we're sat in on an emergency community meeting. The two of us look like we are nursing hangovers and happen to be sitting on dynamite. Both our eyes are bloodshot. I'm nervously popping the joints of my fingers and Steven is tapping his feet. The auditorium area is cleared, and seats have been put in place. About forty residents turned up but what surprises me is the attendance of Spikeway upper management. This is unprecedented. I suppose a collapsing building and potential lawsuits would do that for you.

What if they knew what was really going on? Last night, after dealing with Steven's incredulity and minor melt down at the prospect of dying, we both went out with five old rat detectors I had stored in the Bat Cave and placed them in the sewage areas. It wasn't much, but it would give me a rough idea of the amount of alien traffic moving under our feet. I had to do something. The company's worry about legal fees and bad press paled in comparison to what was really at stake. Spikeway Housing would go on their wild goose chase while Nikki, Steven, and I tried to get this under control. To them, I was just a small cog in a big wheel, but how I saw things now, I could be the big wheel. Hell, I could be the entire fucking machine.

Steven sits beside me in the community center, just as quiet as I am. His eyes have been opened too. I have never seen so many executive types mixing it up with the people living in the buildings that they provided. They had their time to speak; now, it's the residents and the staff's turn. I recognize the managing director who doesn't look as cool as he does on the website. Today he is sweating. Beside him is the Chief Financial Officer - I had to google his details, that's why I recognized him - and he doesn't look comfortable at all.

I'm beginning to wonder why all of these bigwigs decided to leave their ivory towers and come to a meeting like this. They are baring their naked chest to the arrows of the natives. And yet, here they are. Introducing herself as the customer experience manager - I didn't know we had one or even what the role entailed - was the very well put together Maggie Mackintosh. Now this woman has her emotions in check. She is confident answering questions in her boathouse and isn't averse to wandering into other areas of expertise if she has to. Most of the questions are coming from the hand-picked residents. There is no aggression, just mounting concern for their safety and the need for reassurance.

"Rumors are circulating that Spikeway Housing was cutting corners when they were building these properties?" Miss Sohul from Fairview House asks.

The MD takes this question immediately.

"That's just not true, Miss...."

"Sohul," Miss Sohul completes.

"Miss Sohul, our quality control when it comes to these properties was exemplary, and I have the paperwork to prove it," he pauses. "But I want to leave no stone unturned, and an examination of the buildings will take place by an independent structural engineering firm."

"Will we have access to that report?" A tall gaunt man asks, Mr. Truman from Pinner House.

"Of course," the MD says without hesitation.

A hand rises in the middle of the gathered residents. It's Miss Wentworth with her immaculately behaved baby in her arms.

"Shouldn't we be preparing…" she considers what to say next, "if it happens again."

"I can assure you that was an unfortunate one-off," the MD says. "Something like this is unprecedented. The chance of a repeat is remote."

"Are you saying we should wait? Be taken by surprise like we were two days ago?"

The MD leans into the microphone on stage, but Maggie Mackintosh beats him to the punch and rests her elegant fingers over the sponge of the microphone. It makes a popping sound. The MD hesitates while she speaks close to his ear. He nods once and then twice, steps back from the microphone, letting the customer experience manager take his place.

"I think," Maggie says, her voice steady and confident, "I think you're right. We do need an emergency plan in place. And I promise," she looks over to the executive team, "with my colleagues, we can come up with something workable in the next few days. And then something more permanent in the foreseeable future."

For a moment, there is silence, then the small gathering begins applauding. I feel like jumping up and telling them all that they should evacuate the estate now. Telling them that their lives are at stake from a bona fide extraterrestrial invasion from creatures with weird deadly abilities that are ripping the estate apart. Now wouldn't that be stupid? It will get me nowhere. An alien-human coalition is about to be formed. The neighborhood watch won't be happy, but this is out of their league. I look over to Steven and nudge him in the ribs. He looks pasty white and nervous. He is thinking what I'm thinking.

"We got work to do, mate," I say to him.

I don't think he wants me to see or hear his reaction, but his nervous gulp and the gurgle of his stomach speaks volumes.

21.

Later that day, I sit with Steven and the new addition to our merry band, Thomas Prescott. He's the Sewage Engineer who helped me with my rat problem a few years back. We spent some time together on the project, so I know he is into strange shit, and with his sewage expertise, he is perfect. I let Nikki handle the recruitment this time, and she closed the deal in half an hour. So here we are.

We're seated comfortably like kids in the classroom, watching Nikki prepare a presentation of sorts. I made sure all the doors and windows were locked and secured. And for good measure, the door into our restroom is locked too. I may be acting hyper-vigilant, but I think it's justified because of the nature of what we are doing.

So, I'm sitting with my boys, and Nikki has center stage. She must think I'm nuts or be wondering how peculiar humans are. I just can't help staring at her lips, her teeth, how her tongue moves in her mouth when she spoke. Nikki is alien, and I'm stupidly expecting to see something wonderfully strange that will confirm what she is, but there is no chink in her super-sophisticated camouflage. It's flawless.

She looks like a beautiful mixed-race woman who has suddenly grown in stature in my eyes. For the tenth time, I wonder what she really looks like under the CamoTech. I try not to speculate, but I can't help it.

"We will form two teams," Nikki says. "Prescott and I, Clayton and Steven. Our objective is to find and disable the Omni-Seed." She pauses for effect. "The Omni-Seed is not capable of mobility, but it can psionically marshal help from other organisms it controls to move it to the safest zone possible so it can do the most damage."

I should be focused on what Nikki is saying, instead, I'm watching her move. The strength of her legs in the jumpsuit, the curve of her hips, her arse, her waist, and bust. And when I'm done having lecherous thoughts on a woman that is not a woman at all, at least in the traditional sense, my attention is on the duffel bag she carried in like it was nothing. I couldn't see much, but what I did see and kept seeing was enough to fuel my imagination.

Nikki brought the big guns with her.

"You've been looking for it for a while now; how are we meant to find it? What has changed?"

Nikki stops her pacing and looks at me. At that moment, she looks human but feels utterly alien.

"Excellent question, Clayton. It still won't be easy, but we have something to our advantage."

"What?" Prescott asks, knowing the answer would come, regardless of his participation.

"I have the luxury of knowing the Omni-Seed is in an area that I have become very familiar with; I also know everything I did to acquire it in the first place. Before now, I had to keep my activities covert."

I almost raise my hand.

"I know the reason," I sound like an excited kid. "You had to keep your identity secret, so if you had any bigger plans, more radical solutions, applying it without drawing attention to yourself would have been difficult."

"Exactly," she says. "Things are different now. I have…" She thinks about her answer, her mouth moving as if she is testing the words before she says them. "I have you gentlemen to help make this happen."

All three of us nod.

"Something is bothering me," Steven says.

Nikki nods to him, acknowledging his comment. All eyes are on Steven, and he begins a little self-conscious shuffling in his chair.

"I know you said you didn't want to draw attention to yourself, but why?" he asks. "You could have come in guns blazing, found this Omni-Seed thingy and destroyed it. Who cares what we think? Problem solved. End of."

Nikki folds her arms and processes for a moment. She could easily have vaporized Steven's arse for asking a difficult question. I smile at the thought; she doesn't.

"There are billions of civilizations in the universe," she says.

My ears prick up. Nikki must have seen my sudden interest and corrects herself.

"The known universe," she adds. "Many other civilizations know of your existence, but for your own good, we choose not to interfere. You are one of many millions. Your time will come soon. For now, star system Sol Y2591 must not be exposed to cultures or technology from any species that belongs to the 65.5 - kilo parsec system alliance."

"That's a mouthful," Prescott says.

Nikki continues.

"When translated 65.5 refers to the distance from end to end of our galaxy using an Earth astronomical unit of distance for clarity. Your astrophysicists would call us a Pin Wheel Galaxy. All the alliance members exist within that boundary. Penalties are harsh for doing what I've done. I'm risking everything to clear up this mess as quietly and as cleanly as possible."

"You're going to be in the shit when you get back home," Prescott says.

Nikki considers the question, or was it her translation technology processing subtext. I wonder how her high-tech linguistic program could handle a Brummie accent?

"I'd be in 'the shit' for sure. I couldn't return home without this being resolved. Our scientists are waiting to prove or disprove a theory that the Omni-Seed was engineered by a terrorist group," she says. "One of the many factions who stand against our way of life."

"You have them in your world too?" Steven asks, surprised.

Nikki nods.

"Not everyone sees the benefits of an intergalactic alliance."

Prescott clears his throat.

"How does this Omni-Seed protect itself then? Every animal I know needs something if it gets into trouble."

Nikki purses her lips, and I'm impressed with how her command of human gestures are getting better. She looks at Prescott steadily, her eyes flitting to me, checking my reaction, I suppose.

Then she says, "We've thoroughly studied this species, and although there is much we don't know about it, we know it's astonishingly resilient. Its power to mutate and control organisms has a finite distance. But within that area, it has control over its creations and can send them on missions or use them to protect itself. For every rotation of your planet, that communication gets stronger."

Looking around to each of us for more questions and realizing there are none, she pulls the duffel bag into the center of the room. She opens it up and starts unpacking the equipment inside, laying them neatly on the floor. It seems weapons look similar no matter the alien civilization, although I can't see triggers on any of them. Nikki picks up one of the weapons and holds it out. I should be listening to what she is saying, I'm too enamored by what she has in her hand.

"We all need one of these," she says. "I have taken the liberty to calibrate them to your human biology. This should do the job effectively."

"What is the job? Prescott asks. "Are we killing these things or what?"

Nikki's eyes glint with amusement.

"Not on purpose," she says. "I'm already in trouble with the galactic authority as it is. Giving you killing weapons would be a step too far. We need the

Omni-Seed first and foremost. We trap it in a force bubble until it can be transported back to my craft. Ancillary creatures in our way will be disabled by the weapon.

"Correct me if I'm wrong, Nikki," Steven makes a face, "but you've been looking for this Omni-Seed for almost two weeks. There can't be too many places it could be, and you've found nothing. Are you sure it's here?"

"As sure as I can be. From our observation of it on the planet it was taken from, the influence it has over lifeforms was limited to a specific area. It was like it used the space as a test zone first. Then went on to further afield."

"How hard was it to track?" Prescott asks.

"Challenging," she says diplomatically. "It lived on a jungle planet, with gravity twice your planet's own."

"You would think this would be easy-peasy," Steven states, "but it's managed to stay one step ahead of you every time."

"That is the worrying thing. I'm hoping we can find it with our combined efforts."

“I think it’s smarter than you give it credit,” I say. “It’s not just adapting to our environment, it’s learning new tricks.”

“Even if it’s super smart, this is still our manor,” Steven says. “We know every nook and cranny of this estate. If it’s anywhere here, we can find it.”

Nikki hefts the weapon to her shoulder, closes one eye, and spies an imaginary target through a scope that slides smoothly out of stock. She wedges it in the crook of her shoulder and moves the dangerous end around the room. The weapon lights up and issues continuous bars of sound that change pitch as her target changes. When the sight falls on any of the boys, the sound is more piercing. Prescott looks uncomfortable as he becomes the focus of Nikki’s attention.

“It will not hurt human targets but will violently disable all other living things.”

Unexpectedly, she fires a burst at the toaster. The sound is like a harsh bark, and the appliance suddenly disappears in multicolored spears of light. As slowly as it dissipated, the grimy toaster breaks up into hundreds of its constituent parts all floating in a light cloud. Nikki’s fingers dances over the breach of her weapon again, and as her touches produces a melody, the light cloud bursts and the parts explode to the floor.

"I have some extras included," Nikki pats the weapon, waving us closer. "So let me show you how your weapons work."

22.

"I passed three police cars, loads of coppers, and an ambulance in the Mickey D's car park today," Steven says in passing, but the statement feels more loaded than he would like to admit.

"Did you see the body?" I ask.

Steven nods grimly.

"They did their best to shield it from the looky-Lou's. I don't think CSI had turned up yet."

The fast food restaurant is ten minutes' walk from the estate. So, when I utter a knowing 'hmm' as we walk away from the Bat Cave and the community center, our work done for the day, he knows where I was coming from.

We've been on edge all day. On top of our normal duties, our eyes are peeled for strange occurrences. We've been checking rat detectors, noting any residents' bizarre stories, checking possible hiding places, and hoping we can construct a picture of its next moves. We're both dog tired, but neither of us drives, so Steven is walking to the bus stop, and I will be heading home in the same direction. We'll be back early morning again, and Nikki will cover the nightshift.

She isn't physically here; she is using her technology to monitor the entire estate. It feels like Nikki is more prepared from a distance than we ever could be here. We both saunter in silence for a moment; I know what he is thinking, and just like me, he is afraid to broach the question. It feels as if once expressed, it will be like a magic spell, out into the world, making shit happen.

I can't just say nothing. In this regard, I am a lot like my mom; better in than out, she would say. Keeping that burning question to myself isn't an option. It's in the process of leaving the mind to the tongue when Steven says it in a whisper. Even he instinctively feels the power of his words can be less effective by lowering his voice.

"Do you think one of these lot got loose?"

Our steady pace and casual demeanor that has been massaged into our muscles from a busy day suddenly loses its rhythm, and everything feels out of whack. I adjust the backpack around my shoulders, but it still feels uncomfortable.

"I don't think so," I say. "We hardly have any ET activity in the day."

"Your professional opinion?" Steven asks.

My smile is brief and harder to see as evening transitions to nighttime. We walk beside one of the main roundabouts on the estate and slow down.

"Let's think about it," I stop. "From what Nikki said, this Omni-Seed is very territorial. It's gonna stick to a zone, evolve…" I pause for effect, "or devolve the life around it, and when it has full control, it will spread its influence." I sound like I'm reading from a textbook.

Steven nods, and we started walking again.

"I wonder what the ETA on that will be? I mean the end of the world." He says it so casually, as if Armageddon is no big thing.

I shrug, my expression glum.

"Nikki has the answer to that, but she's not sharing."

We walk some more, cutting through a small park with a climbing frame and what was supposed to be a rock feature but became a nocturnal gathering point for the Gen Z weed heads. I push through the creaky gate, noting I need some WD-40 for it tomorrow, and join the footpath that veers off to the estate's small parade of shops. We brush past Mr. Amin doing his rounds, mumbling to himself. He always wears a white jumper and flannel PJs. Like Zuckerberg's T-shirts, Mr. Amin must have a collection of them. His carer will soon realize he is missing and come running.

Just as we reach the corner of the shops, some of the streetlights flicker on. The shadows begin to coalesce in the spots where the light cannot reach. Steven perks up on seeing the colorful dot matrix display of Ali's outpost.

"I'm gonna get a drink from Ali's, my treat. What do you fancy?"

"Get me, a Perrier," I say.

"Posh," he teases. "The Dom Perignon of sparkling water."

I'm mentally poised to correct his facts when my eyes catch movement above me. Steven is already pushing his way into the convenience store as my head tilts up just in time to see a sizeable smudgy silhouette glide or jump the gap between the building that houses the gym and the facility that make up the commercial units.

My eyes follow it as everything suddenly slows down from my perspective just up to the point when the black blob slams into the back of the building, miscalculating its jump. It's frantically scrambling on the vertical face, trying to gain purchase, but it can't. Gravity snatches it, and as it hurtles back to earth, it rips out satellite dishes attached to the wall. Whatever it is, it ends up in a skip with a resounding boom.

Comically, the metal lid closes after its clumsy arrival. The cowardly part of me wants to leg it, leave whatever has fallen inside to make its own way out, if it survived. I just can't. I don't allow fear to paralyze me. I hurry up to the skip, its occupant dazed from the fall but struggling inside. A whiff of rotten food makes my eyes water. I sense a powerful body moving inside the metal garbage receptacle every time it shifts within. There is a large thick bolt hanging from a rusty chain attached to one side of the bin, which is supposed to fit into an equally robust-looking metal ring welded to the lip of the container.

I quickly slip the bolt into the metal ring and step back.

The side of the skip dents violently from impact inside; the paint flakes from the surface with every impact, like a bass drum.

Boom!

Boom!

I flinch and shuffle backward some more, bumping into Steven.

"What?" Steven asks the question with his eyes wide as I point to the skip, my fingers trembling.

"Something fell into the skip," I say, pointing up and over. "It's trying to get out."

"What's trying to get out?" Steven asks.

"I just told you I don't know. I locked it in. It just happened."

Boom!

Boom!

Steven jumps this time, grabbing my arm and squeezing.

"Let's fucking get out of here," his voice is insistent as he stares at me. "We're not ready for this shit."

"I can't just go, Steven. What if it gets loose?" My decision-making muscle is working overtime, and so is my conscience. "I'm responsible, and I think I pissed it off."

"Call Nikki," Steven says like he is out of breath. "This is important, she'll come."

Steven is a good friend. He has my back, without a doubt. Volunteering for the complex and risky stuff is not his forte. And neither is he the man with the plan. But sometimes, just sometimes, he can view a problem from an obtuse angle, something that should have been apparent to you, but you missed completely.

Call Nikki.

The skip explodes into a flurry of bangs, the metal dimpling from the impact on the inside, and we both jump back like schoolgirls. I dig into my pockets and shakily dial Nikki. On three rings, she picks up.

23.

I feel groggy from not enough sleep after overseeing the ET trapped in the dumpster last night. Nikki wanted an early start too and asked me to drive her van. I was wondering if her two-week experience of driving fossil fuel-guzzling Earth vehicles had scarred her. Well, she was about to enjoy the driving skills of my two years of lessons, one theory test and two failed practical exams. I was a bit rusty. Since passing my driving test and getting my grubby hands on a license seven months ago, this is the tenth time I have been behind a steering wheel.

And, yes, I've been counting.

Other than the inability to find fourth gear from

time to time, I'm doing okay. I'm basking in my skills when Nikki places her hand on my knee.

"Turn left here," she says. "And pull up on the right."

I obey.

My parking isn't perfect but good enough. I release my seatbelt, and we both sit staring ahead. From the corner of my eye, Nikki's form shimmers for a moment; her mimic systems unable to completely trick my optic nerves. She has explained to me it's some weird anomaly that must run in my family.

"I have a question for you," Nikki says.

"Shoot," I reply, wondering what is on her mind.

"One of your motorists angrily shouted from his conveyance that I was a black bitch. My data banks understand it's derogatory, but why?"

I shake my head grimly. Being in the presence of an extraterrestrial and saying this makes it sound even more ludicrous.

"In Earth's past, a whole generation of my people were enslaved, murdered, and brutalized as slaves for centuries."

"The Transatlantic Slave Trade," Nikki notes.

"Your people?"

"People with an African heritage," I say.

Nikki looks confused. It's a strange look for her.

"My data says that the present form of the human species all began in the continent you call Africa; therefore, aren't you all Africans?"

"Crazy, right?" I laugh.

She nods.

"We can be irrational, destructive, prejudiced, and cruel, but personally, I think some of us are learning the lessons while others would like the sins of history to repeat itself. Like that wanker in the car."

"Did the perpetrators of the Transatlantic Slave Trade apologize for their transgressions? Reconciliation is the only way to heal," Nikki says. "Our people had to face that truth too."

My laugh now is bitter and filled with the bloody mind pictures I create of what my ancestors had to endure.

"Never. And the only reason why we're talking about this is that you chose a human form that normally would be a mix of African and European blood."

"Blood?" Her brow rises.

"Genetic material," I add. "Once you have African blood, no matter what other ethnic group shares your makeup, you are considered black in many cultures."

"Black is the absence of light, the primordial stuff. The omnipotent clay my people believe makes up the universe." She pauses. "I'm proud to be considered black."

I tear up. Call me a wuss, I don't care. I'm touched.

"Why did you choose this form?" I ask. "You could have been anyone."

"We have a saying on our worlds," she processes the idea for a second or so, "that roughly translates, you know, the sweetness of the flowers from the aroma carried on the wind."

Woah! That sounds suspiciously Caribbean, I'm thinking - a few words of Patois here and there, and it's something my grandmother would have said.

Nikki keeps going. "I felt a kinship with her and understand the struggle your female kind had to go through to be equal. I combined the physical attributes from historical women who lived in the United Kingdom, the United States and Africa."

I'm blown away right now, but I try not to show it except for a sniffle and the widening of my eyes to prevent a tear or two from escaping. We sit in silence for a moment.

"What next?" I ask.

"Now, you become one of the few humans in your short existence on this planet to venture into an alien spacecraft."

"I'm not sure whether I should be scared or pissed off," I mutter.

"A little of both," Nikki says with a straight face.

I think I should tell her about the human preoccupation with being abducted by aliens. Now that I know a bona fide alien myself, it would just sound like we are a perverted species. I don't want to be the one to give our planet a reputation.

I keep my mouth shut on that issue.

"Let's go and poke around the dead bodies of some mutated Earth creatures."

"Let's," Nikki said, lacking enthusiasm and as deadpan as ever.

I conclude her species aren't so hot on sarcasm.

At this very moment, my senses are on overload. I'm trying to stay focused, and it's not working. Nikki leads me over to the empty field, close to where we are parked; the piece of land that stretches from the main road towards the vast arches of the aqueduct in the distance. The same aqueducts the Victorians had built allowing today's high-speed trains to rocket across them. All the way across the tall grass, I tell myself I can do this.

Nikki's scout craft is invisible and floating about a hundred feet above the ground. When I see the ramp materialize like a staircase to heaven, I realize I'm doing this even if my heart is threatening to leap out of my chest. I feel a bit lightheaded, but it passes. I follow behind Nikki, leaving everything I have known to be true in my life and entering the utterly fantastic new world. I walk through a bank of flashing lights which Nikki explains to me are decontamination flares. She doesn't want me leaving any nasty Earth bugs on her ride.

My perception of what to expect of an alien spacecraft has been colored by years of sci-fi movies which, on quick inspection, are primarily wrong. It's a practical interior, nothing abundantly shiny or leathery, but it's functional in a used kind of way. My human biases compare what I'm used to as a human being with how an alien would conceive it. I can't see any storage facilities, no chairs, tables, or anything recognizable. The instrumentation must be hidden because I see nothing that remotely resembles dials, knobs, or meters. Nikki strides confidently ahead of me, her slender arms gracefully reaching above her head, touching or gesturing to something. It makes me look up too.

Wow!

There's more stuff above me, and I suddenly realize the idea of up and down is different from Nikki's perspective.

"I think this is going to feel strange, but you'll get used to it," Nikki says. "Hang on and don't puke in my vessel."

Nikki looks at the back of her hand as a chain of holo-symbols encircle her wrist like a bangle made from light. She reaches out to touch one of the strange characters, watches it react to the tip of her finger and then scrolls through the options before she stops at one and double clicks it.

Suddenly, what was up becomes down, and what was down becomes up. It isn't just a shift in perspective but an actual shift in gravity. I feel like I'm on a Rubik's Cube, where the forces of nature are interacting with me from the x, y, and z-axis all at once. The concept of gravity instantly disappears, and I'm left with the sensation of freedom even though I have misplaced my stomach somewhere I can't find. Incredibly, now I can walk not just on the floor but on what I initially thought was the ceiling and is now the wall. Or is that the floor? No, the wall. Shit!

"How?" I ask.

"You said you wanted to know more about me. Welcome to my perspective. This is how I experience what you call gravity on my planet; force impacts us on multiple plains at once. One of the reasons our species are tripodal."

I look at her, trying my damnedest to see how that would work.

"You could have at least prepared me," I whine.

"That wouldn't be any…"

The sound she utters after the word 'any' is a high-pitched mewl punctured by three distinct shotgun clicks ending with a shrill whistle. A sound no human vocal cord could ever hope to reproduce.

"Huh!" I say, puzzled.

"My apologies," Nikki corrects herself. "I meant to say that would not be any FUN!"

"Earth humor," I say, nodding. "That's cute."

A bead of sweat trickles down the canyon of my back, and the simultaneous itch on my calf makes me twist to reach down to scratch. I'm doing a great job of it. You should try scratching in a hazmat suit.

Precisely.

Nikki, who stands beside me in her curve-hugging flight suit, takes a quick look at my comic performance and stares back into the autopsy room. It hadn't been there earlier but had simply formed in a space Nikki requested. Inside a transparent box is what looks like a black crystalline slab of rock; the body of the creature that fell into the skip last night. Nikki came to save the day, and here it is, all laid out. At either end of the weirdly shaped surgical table are spider-like machines. Their multiple limbs are equipped with cutting, splicing, and suturing extensions. They observe and record the entire process, feeding the data directly to Nikki who explains it to me in human layman terms.

"This was once..." She pauses; her eyes look off into the distance, and they focus again. "Feline domesticus."

"A cat!" I burst out. "But how? Look at that thing."

It's just under five feet long, slender, and muscular. If this thing was a cat in a former life, it had adapted itself not just to mice and rats but with bigger, more challenging prey in mind.

"It looks almost reptilian, those retractable claws and that jaw..."

"Mammalian, reptilian, and the DNA of a cactus," Nikki says.

"How can it do that?" I ask more out of frustration than expecting an answer. "How can it adapt, mix and match the genetic makeup of living things so quickly?"

"The Omni-Seed is a mystery. We know what it does but not how it does it. That's the reason we secured the specimen to study."

"Fighting these things without knowing more about them is going to be impossible." The volume of my voice inches up, and my hands are getting more expressive.

Nikki looks at me in that strange sort of way, as if she is processing what I'm saying and how I feel.

"I'm not saying we have nothing. I'm just saying we don't know enough about it."

I encourage her to keep going with a gesture of my hand.

"The Omni-Seed transmits its commands through a high-frequency carrier wave or exotic subatomic particles that have remained undetectable to us so far."

I shake my head, lines in my forehead thicken with frustration.

"So, wherever it is, it can continue to do its damage undetected?"

Nikki nods.

"That is what makes this particular lifeform so dangerous and interesting."

I'm trying to take all of this in when my phone rings, startling me for a moment. I keep promising myself I will change my Vybz Kartel - Ramping Shop ringtone, but I haven't gotten around to it yet. My eyes remain on the body for a moment as the procedure takes place, but I can't help glancing down when it rings again. I have no intention of answering, but my reaction is just habit. I look back to the cadaver with its flayed skin and exposed internal organs spasming in time with my ringtone.

It can't be, I tell myself, a chill zigzagging down my spine.

The phone rings again.

The cadaver spasms again.

My phone repeats its ring, and the eviscerated creature behind the glass does its shaky dance on the examination table.

I take two steps back, leaving Nikki unmoved ahead of me, peering with interest at the reaction and scrutinizing the tablet.

"I thought you said it was dead," I squeeze the words out of my mouth. "That does not look dead."

"It is," Nikki's voice is small and confident. "Brain function and circulatory function are at zero. But that reaction was…unexpected."

"Unexpected is not the word I'd use for my heart jumping out of my mouth. Unexpected how?"

Nikki looks me up and down and manufactures a half-smile on her beautiful lips, then point-blank ignores me.

"What kind of music was that playing on your phone?"

I wonder if she doesn't have a database of Earth cultural music she can refer to.

"It's Dancehall, popular music from an island called Jamaica. My parents were born there."

Nikki stands stock-still for a moment, processing in the way she does. And then she stares at me, and the eyes of her human form sparkles.

"I think you may have stumbled across something useful."

I look at her dumbly.

"Glad to help, but what did I discover?"

She sighs.

"Our dead friend has a secondary neural network that responds to certain audio tones even after its primary functions are destroyed. It may be something we can use against it or even use to track it. Let me look some more into it; we will see."

I nod to myself, and a glow of satisfaction envelopes me. I'm starting to think I'm a natural at this pest control thing, whether earthbound or extraterrestrial. Then the enormity of it all smothers me.

Nikki must have seen my shoulders slump.

"You have questions about what our next steps are?" Nikki asks.

I nod.

Nikki sighs and I'm amazed at how much of a good job her programming or whatever it is inside her that handles human gestures is performing. I love watching her navigate the emotional landscape we take for granted even if I have a feeling what she is about to tell me is important.

"I know more about the Omni-Seed than I've disclosed to you. I didn't want to cause unnecessary anguish around a situation you couldn't directly control."

I'm not pissed, but I want to know what she knows.

"What do I need to know?" I ask.

"The Seed has a development period when it attempts to take root on a planet. The stages are early, mid and late. In the early stages, it catalogues indigenous species and experiments with transformation and manipulation. In the mid stage, it starts to organize the species it feels are useful and begins its campaign. There is no turning back after that. Its influence begins to grow exponentially. It relies on a range of environmental factors that trigger this stage including energy availability, light, and temperature. These factors are all linked in a complex network that I've been able to decode. Tomorrow will be my last chance to stop this. When it transitions to the late stage, it's at its weakest. This will be our only opportunity.

My chest feels hollow and my mouth desert dry.

"Our last chance," I say.

"Our last chance," Nikki confirms.

I take a deep, stuttering breath as the reality dawns on me.

"You need to send everything you have that I can use to my laptop. You can't do this without our help. You may think this is out of our league, and you may be right, but that has never stopped humans before. We will surprise you."

"If there is any time, I've needed to be proven wrong, now would be a good time," she says.

It's my turn to look at her and wonder what she thinks our chances are. Why do I feel like I'm representing the whole human race? And if I'm, I can't make my ET guest think I'm chicken shit. I have a planet to represent.

"Well," I say, "prepare to be proven wrong."

24.

Soon after Nikki and I leave the scout ship, I start making calls to our ragtag team. All day and into the next night, I make plans using my knowledge and intuition and the empirical facts Nikki sent me.

It's now or never.

The time has come, and I'm nervous as fuck. Just seeing it happen is a surreal thing. Knowing it must happen is what is scary. I can feel the Spikeway Housing Estate losing its grip to an insidious alien army. Residents, dogs, cats, and even Deliveroo riders are disappearing. Residents are scared, and sightings of creatures stalking the grounds day and night are becoming more prevalent. When three more residents disappeared and a duo of community officers never completed their shift after patrolling the estate, we couldn't continue the way we were. As my cousin Omar in Brooklyn would say, shit got real.

If you can believe it, I'm more worried that the local news agencies are beginning to take notice of the stories. Not that Joe Blogg would believe any of this, but the government would. And no, that's not my conspiracy theory. It's a fact as Nikki has GCHQ under surveillance, and from the chatter, it was something MI5 paid attention to. Nikki is controlling the flow of information for now, breaking into secure systems and creating virtual characters in positions of power to maintain the pretense that all is being handled.

We are trying to keep this operation hush-hush, but I have a feeling the Omni-Seed knows we are out looking for it. And if that is the case, what would it do about it. I have considered the residents and the possible fallout this course of action would have on them. I circulated some flyers encouraging residents to stay inside tonight with a cock and bull story of an escaped rabid wolf on its way to a veterinary specialist. Nikki helped by sending SMS messages to every mobile phone on the estate. Without that cover story in place, we would stick out like a pair of albino zebras being hunted by lions.

Steven and I have on medical-grade face masks and goggles, and we are wearing white environmental suits the Housing Association provided us with. On a scale of one to ten protection against corrosive, toxic, or contagious material, I'd say a two-point-five. Beggars can't be choosers. At least we both have the Retro Phase Genome Inhibitors with us, RPG1's for short, and I have a modified night scope slung around my neck. With our kit and enough Dutch courage, I'm hoping it will see three Earth boys through what is about to come knocking. Hope does not feel like a good strategy, but it will have to do. Nikki is the authority on this thing, and as we are risking our lives tracking it down, we all have questions.

Tonight, is the night.

I'm thinking about everything when Steven shoulders me because I've gone all quiet. We stare at each other, looking like a pair of dicks. Steven starts laughing first, and then I join him. We continue guffawing for a while and, with some effort, compose ourselves.

Steven flips up his goggles and wipes his eyes.

"What are you brewing up in that head of yours?" he asks me.

I shrug, self-consciously reluctant to switch up the plan we had come up with together, but I feel this would be better.

"Did you have your Weetabix?" I ask, and Steven looks at me quizzically.

"Yeah…" Steven says, not wanting to fall for the possible verbal trap I'm setting for him.

"Good," I say. "Because I think we should check all the buildings on the estate from Charles Schumer House through to Hummingbird House."

"Oh, man," Steven groans. "That is gonna be a mission. From how Nikki described, this thing is not gonna be on somebody's landing, is it?" Steven yawns for effect, but it does not mask his nervousness. "I think we should stick to our original plan."

I think about it again, and although I can't express my feeling of why I want to do it this way, I reach for a compromise.

"Okay, let's dig around the spots we decided on and swing by some of the flats if we find nothing."

"Lubbly, Jubbly," he says weakly, his happy-go-lucky persona scuffed from fear and needing a spit shine.

I oblige.

"We've got this, mate. Just keep your eyes open."

I look up at a blurry full moon, its face scared with thin wispy clouds gliding across it like spider webs. CCTV cameras have stopped functioning, courtesy of Nikki. The noticeable lack of street illumination is what team Omni-Seed had conjured up but it isn't unexpected. I flip my night scope lenses down over my eyes and watch the world turn radioactive green. We start walking away from the community center, around the corner to Schumer House, but as they say, the best-laid plans.

The night is suddenly split by a scream and then shouts. Our eyes follow the commotion. Residents are fleeing De Beers House. It seems this will be our first call after all.

25.

I intercept one of the people running out of the building, shock in his eyes, chest heaving from shouting or screaming or both. Reducing his mad dash from a bolt to a brisk walk takes me a few strides. I recognize him like I do most residents, but I can't place his name. The man is in his late thirties, skinny, white, and with an unruly mop of hair on his head. I turned to Steven who has been corralled by two panicked neighbors, frightened and firing questions. Our bargain shelf Hazmat suits make us immediate authorities on what has just happened to them. I look back at the man I had grabbed; his white face looks bleached and pallid. The man slaps his hand on my shoulder as if he needs support, and I lean into him to give it.

"They came up through the floorboards. Jesus! What were they?"

I really don't want to open that can of worms, not right now.

I ignore his question.

"Did it happen in your apartment? Is there anyone else with you?"

"With me?" he asks absently, looking over my shoulder one moment and then glancing nervously back from where he had come.

I can't help it, and I follow his eyes to his open door again and the darkened interior. My stomach tightens as I glimpse the frenetic movement inside. It's difficult to see what exactly is happening. They are the size of kittens but not cuddly. Not cuddly at all. They are a nasty mottled brown and centipede-like, but there are hundreds of them, like a termite colony, crawling over each other, going about their business with purpose.

The sound they make isn't loud but is piercing and sits on the periphery of your awareness, drilling into your brain. It reminds me of a macabre version of a bumblebee waggle dance and the accompanying Flight of the Bumblebee concerto playing in my head. I want to walk away, but something is urging me to stay and watch the entire performance to the end. And it's coming.

I squint and begin to see thick gelatinous strands being attached to various points on the door frame. Something is excreting the substances while others frenetically apply it. Within moments, the open door is blocked by a sticky membranous barrier that, as the creatures inside rub against it, makes a sound like a drum skin being scratched. I shudder and step back, breaking the spell.

"Mate," I say to Steven. "You're going to have to get them to the community center. It's the safest place we've got. Who knows what else is coming out of the woodwork?" I pause and think about that. "Have you got the keys?" I ask.

Steven immediately starts patting himself down, then finally looks over to me with a grin.

"Of course, I've got keys," he says, slapping his pockets like he is in an insurance ad.

"Get everybody over there, and when you're

done, call me," I say.

"What are you going to be doing?" Steven asks.

"Our objective hasn't changed. Continue the search. Find the Omni-Seed." I mean to say it with bullet-proof conviction, but to my ears, it doesn't come out sounding like that at all. "We'll meet up later. We're on the clock."

"You're sure?" Steven asks, unable to completely erase the relief from his tone.

"I'm sure."

26.

I look into the twilight world of the estate I've worked at for three years, and everything feels different. This is no longer a place to lay down roots and call home; this is an urban jungle occupied by alien creatures who want to make it their habitat. The Omni-Seed is at its weakest and Nikki is counting on it to make mistakes. We just have to hit it with everything we have.

It's about eleven-thirty as I hurry down Shipton drive. The streetlights here are dim and tired. Every seven sets of metal poles is a 360° CCTV camera post standing like guard towers, silently recording. What they will capture and what is actually happening will be completely different. Nikki has seen to that.

I start to think that if I had the backing of the Housing Association or someone in a position of power who believes in what is happening, we would have approached this differently. Firstly I would have evacuated all the accommodations. It would have been a task, but possible. And also an additional ten teams scouring the buildings and landscapes for the Omni-Seed.

Wishful thinking.

I adjust the strap attached to my RPG1 and let it rest more comfortably on my hip, ready for anything.

Well, that's what I tell myself.

I come off the main road just in front of Minion House and follow the footpath that is two flagstones wide, lit by insipid yellow bulbs along the apartment building wall, circling it to the back. I look over to the allotment stretched out into the gloom, fenced, gated, and eerie like a cemetery. It's quiet. Again I adjust the RPGI strap over my shoulder and reach into the pocket of my jumpsuit. I grip the meter Nikki designed from the shell of a mobile phone and pull it out to look at the luminescent screen.

I'm trying to remember if Nikki gave the weird-shaped instrument a name, but what I do remember is its reach is shit. Not my words, Nikki's - she was getting good at this human vernacular thing. We need to be at least twenty-five feet from the Omni-Seed to detect its presence, but in its weakened state, a hundred feet. Although I'm not looking forward to rummaging through vegetables in the dark, this is about being thorough.

I let out another sigh and proceed to open the swing gate. It creaks, and I cringe. That's when I hear it, a ghostly dirge of sirens that I immediately feel will be coming here before the night is over. I stop and wonder what kind of negative self-talk I'm exposing myself to and start singing a Bob Marley tune. I step into the allotment and peer over my shoulders, double-checking I'm not being followed.

I'm alone.

Except…

There is another sound that makes my stomach tighten. It's faint at first but becomes more insistent the longer I hear it. It's like a starved puppy enjoying scraps, interspersed with electrical crackles and pops. I hesitate for a moment. Torn between wandering around the darkened allotment and investigating this new sound, guess what I decide on?

I close the gate behind me and made my way back to where I came from, straining my hearing to pick up the origins of the sound. I come out to the front of Minion House, and I'm expecting the sound to be louder, but it still hovers on the edge of my awareness. The hungry slurping, the electrical discharge, and my sense of dread. I quickly take in the estate at night, and it feels off. A woman walking her dog; a biker and a car drive past me; the occupant of one of the flats is drunk and singing at the top of his voice. I want to scream at them and tell them to get off the street and be quiet, but what good would that do.

My thoughts snap back to the task at hand when, for some reason, my eyes focus on a green junction box at the curb to my right. It's one of those telecommunication and internet hubs the Sky engineers regularly open up, laying bare its innards and doing whatever they did to maintain smooth connections. They obviously aren't working tonight, but something else has seen fit to take over their duties.

I swing the RPG1 from my back and grip it; my

heartbeat starting to ramp up in ferocity, and I step towards the vibrating junction box. With every step, I'm beginning to ask myself what the fuck I'm doing. My legs are weak, and I'm trembling, but I push on.

A new sound erupts from inside the box, making me stop. It's part wail, part squeal. It sounds like animals squabbling over food, then something hops on top of the cabinet and flaps its leathery wings. I gulp and would have dropped the RPG1 if it wasn't slung around my neck. I hold my breath; there's a pounding in my head and pins and needles in my feet and hands like I'm tuned in to my body going into defensive mode as my mind is trying to understand what I'm looking at.

It's like a bird but not a bird. Its body is all wrong. It's like something that has been given the ability to fly as an afterthought. It's dark-skinned and hairless and moves on all fours reptilian-like. From the side, I can see its squat neck is thick. It has a hexagonal head and large pointy ears like a goblin. And what looks like, from my angle at least, an insane grin that houses a mouthful of gleaming conical teeth like daggers.

I shudder and feel lightheaded.

This is some animal mutated via Wi-Fi by the Omni-Seed, an intelligent alien mad scientist. On their own accord, my legs shuffle backward, lowering the nozzle of the weapon in my hand. My heel catches an empty can of lager and makes a loud scraping sound. The creatures look up, disturbed by it, but continue to argue amongst themselves, and I see their faces much clearer. Another wave of shock slams into me, the hairs on my body stand on end, and a chill settles at the base of my spine, churning my guts like I had diarrhea.

In its odd-shaped head, where eyes should have been is a gash that glows red. It's as if its insides are an infernal fire that peeks through a grate in a hellish furnace. Another one of its kind joins the indignant squabbling, then another and another. Luckily, my clumsiness with the can goes unpunished, but how long will my luck hold out. I take it as a sign someone wants me around a little longer, and I keep moving back towards the shadow cast by Minion House.

I don't stop until my lower back connects with what feels like an iron railing. I shuffle right, exhausting the support to my back, and only then do I turn around and hustle into the foyer. Breathing hard, my back to the door and feeling safer in here than out there, I peer through the glass of the swing doors, considering my next move. The decision is made for me.

I see the bobbing headlights from what looks like two, no, three mopeds, heading up the road. Their sound is distinctive. Immediately I know who it is, and in five minutes, their path will take them straight past that murder of bat things. I know the trio reprobates, and even they don't deserve what is lying in wait for them. I rush through the foyer to a fire door at the back; I slam the emergency release bar down and shoulder my way through. I run along one of the footpaths that crisscross between buildings and veer left across the carpark, vaulting an easy fence then legging it through a passage that drops me out just before the roundabout. I see them coming, and with my chest heaving, I run out towards them, shouting and waving my arms.

I must look like a right prat, but I don't care.

They do well not to burst out laughing immediately, but the RPG1 gives them pause for thought. My weapon doesn't look remotely fake. Outside of its odd look, they can see it has heft to it and the kind of battered authenticity only a well-used instrument would show. They slow down just long enough for them to recognize who I am. The rider in the green crash helmet opens his big mouth first. I know the wanker as Robbie. Potential Hitler youth member. Not one of my favorite people.

"Who are you supposed to be then?" he asks.

I know another one of the riders as a local boy who I thought had more sense hanging out with these dimwits. Obviously, I was wrong. His comic timing is off, but he is impressed with his own hilarity and is just able to get the words out.

"He's so black, he needs a white suit so he doesn't get run over by traffic."

That gets them all snickering.

I keep the rage in check, knowing none of them individually would step to me like that, but there is strength in numbers.

"You tossers think you're funny," I growl, surprising them with my ferocity. "Okay, I'm going to let that slide. I will chalk it up to too much weed and one too many pints." I look at them in turn, hoping my position and age difference will garner some respect.

It just doesn't matter.

"Don't get shirty with us, bruv, you're the one that looks like a dick. Halloween ain't for months yet."

They start getting comfortable with the situation. They think there's sport to be had here, but I don't have the time or the inclination for this shit.

My eyes flick to their mopeds. One of them looks rough around the ignition, like a blunt instrument had been used to access the circuitry underneath.

I try a different tack.

"Take another route home tonight, or I'll let the Old Bill know you're riding stolen bikes."

My demand doesn't go down well.

"Snitch!" one of them sneers. And that is all it takes.

"Fuck this," Robbie bursts out. "And fuck you."

The group crank up their bikes and shoot off along the route I forbade them to take.

I look in the direction of the junction box, and I'm beginning to hope the cyclopean nightmares had destroyed the innards of the metal box and moved on to fresh pickings. It's a childish habit, I know, but I cross my fingers and mumble a sorry excuse for a prayer. As the sound of their engines recede, divine intervention seems a good strategy. I don't realize it, but I'm holding my breath, then I relax as I can still hear the gurgling engines.

All is good until it isn't.

Why did I think it would go any other way?

A scream punctures the air, and the sound of the mopeds tumbling across the road echoes back to me. There is another shrill shriek and the sound of metal and plastic smashing into something solid and unforgiving. I start running along the road, following the ill-fated route. At first, it's difficult to see what is happening ahead of me because the lights are down. But soon, the carnage becomes crystal clear.

The creatures are naturally camouflaged by night except for some shifting distortions along their flight path. I can hear the wings flapping, their screeching mixed with the screams and panic of the boys. I look up, thinking the hellish things have changed their signature cry, but what meets my eyes makes my blood chill. One of the boys is about sixty feet in the air and coming towards me, carried by a murder of the flying creatures while he flaps and squirms. When the mutations realize his clothes are ripping under his weight, they grab for something that gives them more purchase; his flesh. The boy's eyes bulge, he screams, he gibbers pleas and sobs as his blood splashes to the blacktop.

Drip, drip, drip, splat.

I dare not look at what body part has parted from its owner. I choke back a new sound that wriggles from my throat, and I let it out into the world like disgusting puke. I swing the RPG1 from my back into my awaiting arms, heft it skyward, and tap my three fingers on the irregular stock. There is a weee-thump sound; the smell of ozone envelopes me as a greenish wave spits from the weapon I hold and slams into the distorted air surrounding the boy aloft. I did some damage, I can tell.

The boy's altitude falls as they fly above me. He looks unconscious or dead and is precariously being held from his trousers alone, but almost immediately, more winged creatures replace the ones I had destroyed or incapacitated. I fire again, and they anticipate my attack, changing direction and using a tall spruce tree as cover. They disappear from sight.

"Damn! Damn!" I swear, my voice returning.

More screams coming from the roundabout ahead

galvanize me into action. I start running towards the sounds of fear and pain only to see loudmouth Robbie is swarmed by the things, frantically trying to swat them away. He is overwhelmed. So far, he has done an excellent job of being in a fetal position. They try to hook his flesh, lacerating him all over in their frenzy, but are unable to get enough leverage to lift him skyward. Soon, that won't be a problem.

I fire once, twice, three times, getting the hang of the effect it has, and scatter the creatures in an explosion of screeches and flapping wings. I approach Robbie and kneel beside him. He is still curled up, twitching and groaning but very much alive. His bike hopped a shallow fence and ended on its side, smashing into Mr. Greenford's bushes. The other two bikes lie shattered on the road. One rider has been taken; the other must-have run off into the darkness.

My wandering mind focuses on the situation at hand. Robbie doesn't look good. He is bleeding from bites and scratches all over his body. His jacket and trousers are ripped from the fall and the attack. I can't tell if he has broken bones or not, but I know I can't leave him here. The gears of my mind are turning, and my eyes are peeled as I peer into the shadows for any movement or threat. I must have scared them off for now.

What I should do next comes to me.

If that sounds too cool, like I have it all worked out, then that's wrong because I don't. I can't take him back to the community center, not in his condition, but I think I know where I can take him.

The toe-rag is heavy, and I'm not gonna lie, I want to dump his 'rass' on the sidewalk as we struggle, but Mama French, being the good Christian woman that she is, did not raise me like that. That doesn't mean I can't give him shit on the way.

"You need to lay off the Mickey D's, bruv," I moan. "You ever heard of a balanced diet? I like KFC like the next man, but come on."

Robbie wants to get involved in the tongue lashing, but he's in too much pain to defend himself.

"I'm about to save your miserable life," I pause. "Fingers crossed." I playfully wait for an answer, and when none comes, I say, "You're welcome dickhead."

Out of breath, with Robbie's arm around my

neck, I pull him up to Number 46 Seafront Place and awkwardly press the door buzzer. Robbie collapses further, but I heave him up to a semblance of standing with my last reserves of strength. In moments, the light comes on inside, then the lights outside illuminating his pallid features. The internal lock on the door clicks, and finally, the door swings open.

The tall, elegant figure of Fowsio Hassan, mother of three and chief nurse at the local hospital, stands framed in the doorway. Her hajib isn't as neat as usual, but I have just roused her late at night in her home.

"Mr. French?" Her relaxed facial expression changes to surprise then shock as she sees the bleeding boy standing beside me. "Are you okay?"

"Mrs. Hassan, I need your help."

She processes the request quickly, looks at the bleeding boy, and recognizes him as one who has consistently called her son a sand nigger and camel jockey. The same boy who threatened her when she reported him to the police. The one who is rumored to be a Neo-Nazi and a paid-up member of the banned FKD - Feuerkrieg Division. That same shit groaning in pain and bleeding from numerous vicious bite wounds, is ushered inside her home without a word of complaint.

27.

Nikki reached down to pull Prescott up from the manhole. Not that the Sewage Engineer needed a hand, but Nikki thought it was something she should do. Prescott straightened himself up, dressed in chest high industrial waders, hardhat with super headlights and communication rig of receiver and transmitter. He had walked for about a mile in the sewage network, guided by Nikki from above. It seemed she had been correct, there had been a lot of underground animal traffic to this location.

"They've been busy," Prescott said. "All kinds of tracks, shit and infrastructure damage."

Nikki nodded silently. Her teammate bent back

with hands in his pockets and looked up at the seven-story building of Runnymede House, then looked back at Nikki.

"You think the Omni-Seed is at the top of this building? How did it get up there?"

"You disappoint me," Nikki said. "From my short time here on your planet, I have observed animals dispersing plant seeds by eating them…" Nikki paused, processing, then continued, "and defecating somewhere else, therefore, extending the range of plant habitat. Endozoochory, your scientists call it."

"You're trying to tell me that something swallowed the Omni-Seed as it hitched a ride in the host's gut, brought it to the top of the Runnymede House, and then had a shit."

Prescott laughed and Nikki looked puzzled.

"Metaphorically speaking, yes." Nikki said, her eye sparkling.

She explained. "Instead of covering itself in a sweet or fragrant flesh, encased in skin or shell, the Omni-Seed attracts its minions psionically. The suggestible minds it will use to do its bidding come in all shapes and sizes. It can spread its mutation like your birds but without a digestive tract."

The penny dropped.

"Someone carried it up there," Prescott said. "Why didn't you just say that?"

"I did," Nikki said, her brows lowered in contemplation.

Prescott sighed and watched her as she assessed the building with the sweep of her head, top to bottom, left to right.

"What do you want me to do?" Prescott asked casually, looking down at the RPG1 Nikki had handed him on his return to top side.

"The plan is to retrieve or destroy the Seed before it does any more damage," Nikki stated as if it was obvious.

"Shouldn't we call in Clayton and Steven for backup?" he asked.

"I suspect the Omni-Seed is here because somehow it's blocking all electromagnetic transmission from its perch." She pointed to the roof of the building and slung her weapon back, making it bounce on her arse. "It would have been useful to have the assistance, but what if I'm wrong?" Nikki said. "You all must continue with the mission if I don't make it."

Prescott sighed, his head lowered.

"Okay," he said reluctantly.

"Protect my flank as I enter the building. The Omni-Seed will be protected. It may send its minions, or they may already be in the building. I will neutralize what I can, and you must do the same from down here."

Prescott's Adam's apple bobbed up and down in his neck.

"I've got it," he said.

Nikki glanced at him with an appraising eye.

"I'm…nervous too," she found the appropriate words. "Do your best, but if you lose control of the situation, protect yourself as I showed you. Don't be a 'Drec.' Life is a precious thing."

Prescott smiled weakly, understanding through context what Nikki was alluding to. He swung the RPG1 from his hip to his chest.

"Let's do it."

Nikki nodded and stepped towards the building; something about her shadow was oddly irregular. She reached up to her neck and touched a fancy adornment that covered her shoulders and throat. The alien trinket began an incredible process of manufacturing body armor in real-time around her. In seconds, it wove the exotic material over most of her body except for her head. That was left to another trigger mechanism at the back of her neck which she waved her hand over. Her helmet blossomed open around her head, covering it in a metal-crystalline shell. By the time she opened the door to enter, she was a Space Marine ready for almost anything.

Prescott's mouth fell open.

"Bloody hell, I gotta get one of those."

28.

As if I didn't have enough things to worry about, my eyes were also peeled for flying mutant bats or whatever the fuck those things were in the night sky. After leaving Robbie in the capable hands of Mrs. Hassan, I made my way back to the allotment. With my trusty meter in hand, I waste no time scanning the area and satisfy myself that it's clear of Omni-Seed activity. I'm tempted to head back to the community center for Steven. We are not supposed to be doing this individually, but there is a time element to consider here too. We have to conclude this before morning, one way or the other.

The twenty minutes hustle back to the centre

could be best suited clearing some more places on the list. Since I parted company with Steven earlier, I haven't been able to talk to him. I can't do anything but pray that he stays put until he hears from me. It's dangerous out here. My mind made up, I leave quickly towards the ruined Chapel, spot number two on my list.

A century ago or so, way before this estate was a concept in the mind of a contemporary architect, this section I purposefully make my way through was a piece of open land. Beside the land was an infamous sanitarium with a chapel on its grounds. As time progressed from the early nineteenth century, the Chapel remained a constant landmark, but all around it changed. A hospital was built, the sanitarium became a psychiatric ward, and the land around it became housing stock. It seemed there was no need for religion in the new world of the sixties, and the Chapel fell into disrepair. I have always wondered why they never demolished it; maybe some society earmarked it as a heritage site or a building that needed to be restored to its former glory. Whatever the case, it has been left in a dilapidated state.

The house of worship is draped in scaffolding

and pointing skywards, like a skeletal finger. A giant dust guard swaddles the entire building, preventing the surrounding environment from damage from where it has been shredded by the elements. The material flaps forlornly as gusts of wind blows through it. I shouldn't be spooked, but I am. The hairs on the back of my neck stand on end as every shadow, every murmur startles me. I have a key for the chain padlock that secured the main gate into the restricted area. My mind is starting to question the existence of ghosts, for God's sake. I'd be a fool not to reserve a portion of my newly acquired perspective on the universe for that possibility too.

As I carefully make my way into the ruins, I'm seriously wondering if I can take another shift in my firmly held beliefs if I see a ghost. I shudder at the thought and flick on my head flashlight. The floor space in front of me is ample. I can imagine pews on both sides with the center aisle leading up to what must have been an altar and the stained-glass window with the sign of the cross above that. But what stands before me in the darkness is rubble, weeds, and possible debris from the roof collapsing in on itself. Walking through it in the daytime would have deemed precarious, but at night it's suicidal.

I take my time with the Omni-Seed meter swinging from left to right like I'm an altar boy swinging incense. If I don't break my ankle, I should be finished in twenty minutes. The smell of pigeon shit and vegetation is not a good mix, and the waft of ammonia in some areas makes my eyes water.

I flip the goggles over my eyes.

As nervous as I'm trying to take this in my stride, who am I kidding? This is a once-in-a-lifetime adventure. An event that will define my life if it doesn't kill, maim, or commit me to an insane asylum. I switch my focus back to the luminescent screen of my Omni-Seed meter, and I see something that makes my heart race. The old school dial on the jerry-rigged instrumentation quickly flickers noticeably left and then right and then back to median again. Not that significant, you may think, but I haven't had any activity from it at all as I walked through the estate. I stop and stare, but the needle remains stubbornly in place.

Finally, I take a tentative step, and an area of undergrowth ahead of me to the left explodes into activity. There are screeches, growls, and frenzied struggling under the canopy of weeds. I drop the Omni-Seed meter and let it swing from my belt. I reach for the RPB1, my heart pounding. Before I can start blasting, the undergrowth erupts, and like little pocket rockets, whatever is causing the disturbance flees, shooting off to every corner of the Chapel.

Did I scare them? Or could something else have done that for me? I have to go and see.

"No, you don't." The voice in my head has a dark, selfish edge to it. "You've done enough already, showed everyone you can be the big hero. Now save your own skin, go home and let's call it a night." The tone lowers conspiratorially. "It will be our little secret."

Either I'm tired, or there is something strange in the air messing with my head. I ignore my vocal dark half and pick my way over to the spot of the disturbance. I cautiously shuffle up to the violently disheveled vegetation.

I sneeze.

I couldn't help it, a pungent rankness wafted up from the bushes, but it doesn't last. I peer at the tangle of vines and leaves, not wanting to lose my balance but needing to take a closer look.

I stoop.

My eyes widen.

I wasn't expecting this.

I'm not sure what I was expecting. All nestled up in what could have been a kind of warren is the cutest ball of fluff I have ever seen since Pokémon. I shake my head in amazement.

There is no way this could have been the reason for the hurried departure of the other creatures in the undergrowth. But here it is, purple puffball, the last man standing. This is a species of animal I have never seen before, and I'm a veteran of David Attenborough's Blue Planet. There is something wrong with it. Cute but wrong.

It's the size of a chubby kitten with a platypus type bill, big doe eyes, and long floppy ears. It looks a bit wobbly on its feet with some slashes on its body that dribble blood. At first, it looks up at me, baring teeth and showing them off with a determined growl, but after I placate it with soothing words, it calms, pacing up and down its little paddock. Then, against all common sense, I put my gloved finger in its little enclosure and rub its head and cheeks. I just can't help myself.

It doesn't transform and bite my finger off.

A good sign.

Instead, it snuggled up to my finger and purrs.

I don't know why I imagined that whatever this alien Omni-Seed mutated would be dangerous and definitely not agreeable. I realize it doesn't have absolute control over its creations as I first thought it did. But, this adorable little thing is proof enough that, extraterrestrial or not, if you mess with Mother Nature, she will mess back.

29.

Nikki was in full battle gear. She had been able to avoid direct conflict by not taking the wire propelled conveyance the humans called a lift to the top floor. That would have been tempting fate. Instead, she took the stairs and exited on level six. Nikki stood at the head of the corridor. Fluorescent tubes ran centrally above her and flickered. What light that did enter the space had a dirty green glow from the fittings smeared with gunk she could not identify. It dripped from the ceiling to the floor, carpeting portions of the corridor in pools of viscous fluid.

Nikki wondered if the humans behind the numbered doors were hibernating or just didn't care to investigate what was happening outside. She was glad they chose to remain indifferent. Because whatever had been here before her had been busy marking its territory. Even if she didn't see them, the welcome party was already in place, waiting for her arrival. Nikki made a hand gesture, and her ballistic helmet and rebreather grew out from the housing surrounding her neck, covering her head in a transparent hard shell.

Before she proceeded, she merged her armors CalculeX system with Uncle in geo-synchronous orbit. The sentient computer was Nikki's eyes and ears. Some of its vast computing power was now contained in her exo-skeleton. She took a step forward, knowing the schematics of the building and having checked human life signs with spectrographic analysis and a range of bioelectrical emanation readings. With all the computing power at her disposal, she couldn't know what was in store, just the potential possibilities. She walked carefully towards the door at the end of the corridor, her enhanced senses working under the surface.

She reached for the door at the end of the corridor that would lead to another set of stairs heading up to the last flight of stairs. Nikki couldn't help wondering if she had been as thorough as needed. Did she miss something that would bring this chase to a satisfying end? No time for doubts now. Her hand hovered over the chrome handle, and just as she was attempting to pull it open, she sensed the door imperceptibly rocking in its frame like a loose tooth.

Instinctively, she tucked and rolled, the fire-door tearing off the hinges and swatting her back across the hallway. Nikki skidded to a stop and struggled to her feet, looking back to see the doorframe struggling to contain a writhing, seething mass of dark ectoplasm with whipping gross protuberances slapping on the floor like it was exploring for prey. Nikki used a swing of her hips to bring her RPB1 in front of her. She hefted it, aimed, and tapped her fingers on the stock in one smooth movement. Where the energy blasts impacted, it withdrew with the sound like a squealing Gokkun.

Protecting itself, the organism fired back, letting fly projectile branches of itself, slamming into Nikki's weapon, messing up the shot, and gunking up the processor unit inside the stock. She tried again, but the RPB1 was cycling ineffectually, its self-cleaning program taking too long. The thing in the doorway was firing these razor-sharp extensions of itself, and Nikki was evading them like a warrior dancer.

Every evasive action Nikki took, she got closer to the doorway, but every forward movement was proving difficult. Two more spikes flew at her with a double Pop! Pop! They pinned her hand and foot to the ground. She screamed, reached back to her calf with a free hand; a bladed weapon slid out of a compartment around her leg. Her eager fingers reached for the ornamental grip, and she dragged it out, slashing at the two vines pinning her to the spot. The humming blade cut through them effortlessly, and the stumps pulled back, screeching and wriggling in the seething mass ensconced in the doorway.

Gritting her teeth, Nikki scurried backward. Her alien metabolism repaired her wounds as quickly as it could, but the pain was like being burnt in the molten lakes of her home planet. She rolled to a fighting stance, whipping her knife from one hand to the next, weaving and bobbing, making herself a difficult target to hit. But the creature was done with using Nikki for target practice; it had another trick in mind.

There was a sound that could have come from a latrine, oozing from the creature in the doorway. Nikki's eyes widened as a green bubble formed with a wet gurgle, popping grossly away from the mixed-up genetic material straddling the door, floating in the air, and starting to expand in size. Nikki raised her arms and fired a round of projectiles from a gauntlet forming around her wrists. They hit the approaching bubble flush on, penetrating the thin film and shooting right through to lodge into the walls behind with a Thud! Thud! Thud!

Nikki smiled.

As far as her programs had informed her, it was an unusual human mannerism that was a way of showing happiness on the one hand and a raft of different emotions on the other. No wonder the cultures of this planet had unresolved issues; they couldn't effectively communicate with each other.

Nikki stuck with her interpretation of the curling of her lips and brought her blade front and center. The bubble rushed towards her, expanding as it moved, and Nikki marked the air with her vibrating blade in anticipation. She was seconds away from engaging it when her suit started alerting her with mild but insistent pulses. Information on her Heads-Up Display began to unfold, and the story it told made her scuttle backward. Her exit was blocked, so she might as well keep swinging. But, as her blade sizzled through the air, her efforts had no effect; the bubble engulfed her. Inside it, Nikki knew she was trapped.

30.

I hurry back into the estate feeling like Zelda from Xbox fame, having completed a minor quest and brandishing some magical tool that could prove to be helpful. I'm not at the boss level, but Furball could either help me get there or be a pleasant distraction.

Who knows?

At this moment in time, it looks as threatening as a powderpuff, cooing contentedly in the oversize pocket of my environmental suit. I use two fingers to adjust its position, so it's comfortable. Furball snuggles up to my hand, thinking it's going to get a tummy rub. When that doesn't materialize, it looks at me balefully with those big eyes and floppy ears.

"What am I going to do with you?" I ask it.

It perks up and shifts its position in my pocket excitedly, like a puppy.

"We going to have to find you a good home," I say, but who am I fooling? I can't leave this munchkin in the care of just anyone. It has to be someone I trust implicitly, or I would have to provide it a home myself. I don't even know what it was.

Is it domesticated?

What is its diet?

I'm asking myself all these questions and not realizing I'm already at the back of the small parade of shops that service the residents. This is the third on the list of places I'm supposed to be looking at. It's a bit of a long shot and not really the kind of place the Omni-Seed would hide out, but I want to be thorough. This is where the creature we autopsied had fallen into the skip and an excellent place for others of its ilk to hide short term, especially because of the refuse issues I've been having with the shopkeepers and the Council.

Cardboard boxes, corrugated paper lining, bubble wrap, and various plastics spill out into the alley, making the containers look like they can't keep down their food and are vomiting their contents onto the street. It feels extra dark as I stand at the entrance into the refuse area. All the lights except for one flicker rhythmically and cast agitated shadows, like they are on the verge of giving up the ghost. I turn on my headlight, grip my RPB1, and step into the cubist nightmare of boxes and cardboard. I look down at the Omni-Meter swinging from my belt. The screen is blank and showing no activity.

"Here goes nothing," I say, realizing I'm not the only one feeling a little apprehensive. Furball is making a soft mewling sound. I start wondering if it knows something I don't. I draw an intake of breath and step into the shadows. I swing the RPB1 from left to right, straining my ears for any sounds. The aroma from the bins is a heady mix of moist cardboard and spoiled food. I stop breathing through my nose as I go. Something flutters past my ears, and I instinctively try to swat it away, but because both my hands are occupied, it came off as an awkward shrug and a flick of my head.

That's when I hear the faint moan rise from the ground, and my heartbeat reverberates in my throat.

Panic doesn't have time to register as I feel a hand grip my ankle. The beginning of a squeal rattles from my throat, and I instinctively try to flee, but whatever it is, it holds on for dear life. I grip the RPB1, panic taking root as I swing the butt around and lower myself to pummel whatever holds me.

"It's me, Clayton, it's me," a croaky voice filled with fear drifts up from some wedges of styrofoam. There is another moan, and the voice calling my name makes me hesitate.

Recognition comes to me slowly.

"Steven?" I ask, falling to my knees and frantically digging into the mounds of paper and cardboard to reveal my workmate and buddy looking pale and drawn.

"Mate, what are you doing in here?" I ask him. "Can you stand?" I don't wait for an answer and start pulling him to a sitting position. He grimaces, baring his teeth.

"I was waiting for you…turned up here...saw movement," Steven takes in a ragged breath. "Something in that fucking mess stung me...I couldn't move at first...I'm getting weaker…I didn't want anyone else stumbling into it."

I give Steven the once over and look at the area where the stinger tore his suit through his civvies and into the skin of his thigh.

"Oh shit," I say, not liking the wound. "I need to get you back to the Bat Cave. Do you think you can walk?"

It sounds like a question, but it isn't. I have to get him back to the community center for medical attention. Nikki considered this possibility like any general worth their salt would. I wonder if her alien first aid kit would be effective on human physiology. We never had the time to test it. My boy Steven will have to take one for the team. He nods at me weakly as he reads my mind. Right about now, I need Nikki's counsel, but she is doing her part. I just have an overwhelming urge to know if she is making any progress. Is she okay?

"Let's get you out of here," I say to Steven. I crouch awkwardly and get his arm around my neck. I stand with his entire weight on me and know my squats at the Iron Planet are good for more than cosmetic thighs. He groans, his eyes misty, and holds onto me for support. Thankfully, once he is standing, we share the load.

"I can walk." Steven tries his best to stand straight. His voice is lower and shaky. "I can walk."

"I've got you," I say, and with his arm around my shoulders and me gripping him under his armpit, we begin our shuffle, skirting the shadows back to the Bat Cave.

31.

Prescott checked his watch. Thirty minutes had elapsed, and he has heard nothing from Nikki. He didn't feel right about what he was going to do even if he had been told to. Nikki made him promise to continue with the mission without her. Even when he knew it made sense, and even when he also knew that if Nikki couldn't handle whatever it was she confronted, he had no chance.

Prescott checked his watch again.

He couldn't wait here forever even if he had not been needed to protect her back. Yet still, he wondered. Had he given her enough time before he decided to bug out? Could she be on the verge of stepping out of the building, joining him on the pavement triumphant? He stared at the door, and it stared back. He fidgeted, his heart pounding, although there was nothing around to threaten him other than the shadows. He had looked up to the building so many times, he had lost count. It stood silent as before. Nothing indicated that the subtle takeover was taking place and he was involved in putting an end to it or putting an end to them. Shuddering, he rechecked his watch and made the decision.

Got to go.

He turned his back to the building just as a soundless explosion of bluish-green energy erupted into the night from the top floor. Prescott sensed it in his head, or did he see it from the corner of his eye; he wasn't sure which. Was it a sign of victory or defeat? He took a faltering step and thought about looking back.

He remembered Sunday school, Sodom and Gomorrah. He remembered how that story scared him, imprinted a sense of dread he carried with him even as an adult. Before he realized they were not alone in the universe, he would have said he was being stupid, su-

perstitious. Not now, not after everything he had seen.

He would not look back, but he waited for what felt like many minutes, hoping he would hear her call out to him. Hoping she would tap him on the shoulder and say it was done.

It was not to be.

Prescott set his attention and his jaw straight ahead as he stepped away from the flats. Onwards into the darkness. Onwards into another possible plan because this one, as far as he could see, was fucked.

32.

"Bruv..." Steven's voice is a hoarse whisper. "I think your leg is on fire." I'm so focused on our steps and trying to conserve enough energy to get me to the community center without collapsing from exhaustion that I miss Steven's words the first time.

"What's that, mate?" I ask him.

"Your trousers...on fire," Steven slurs.

I look down at my grimy hazmat suit and slide my eyes over to the pocket Furball inhabits. It's glowing a weak orange-red as if embers are catching into a flame. I stop, my chest rising and falling with the effort I've expended. I look at the sleeping creature in my pocket. There is no uncomfortable heat as if I'm about to burn. All I can feel is a living, breathing creature asleep. Its fur glows, and I glance up at Fenchurch House just in the distance. I turn to Steven.

"I'm fine, but when you're feeling better, I got someone I need to introduce to you."

Confused static flashed across the twin monitors of Steven's eyes. I know my comments are noted, but my friend gets back to the arduous process of walking. I look back to Furball, my new focus point, and try to use that against muscle fatigue. I watch how bright its fur becomes as we march towards Fenchurch House. It's like it's on fire, and I start to squint from the intensity, but as soon as I turn left on Terry Avenue, the intensity begins to fade. The further we get from that building, the more Furball becomes itself again. I'm tired, but my mind is still racing.

This means something.

So much to discover about it. And this is not the right time to ask questions. We have to find the Omni-Seed and we are narrowing down the places it could be. Our plan isn't complex. Search everywhere. It's as simple as that. The search stops only when the Seed is definitively discovered. Then we will all descend on it. So far no one has sounded the alarm. I have to keep going with or without help.

As the questions begin flooding my mind like the speeded-up special effects sequence in a film, I feel the weight of Steven around my shoulders again. Just for a moment, for a blissful moment, my thoughts transport me away from the physical forces of the real world. The community center is in sight about five hundred meters away, lit up like a Diwali celebration. It's a celebration, all right. Alien contact of the third kind. Historical even. And I'm a witness to it. A pity about the alien invasion aspect of it, but beggars can't be choosers.

I don't think it's appropriate, but I feel a sense of satisfaction, carrying with it enough feel-good energy that makes me straighten up, smile at Steven's bleary-eyed gaze, and march towards the finishing line.

* * *

"Bruv...," Steve's voice was a hoarse whisper. "I think your legs on fire." I'm so focused on our steps and trying to conserve enough energy to get me to the community center without collapsing from exhaustion that I miss Steve's words the first time.

"What's that, mate?" I ask him.

"Your trousers… On fire," Steve said again.

I look down on my grimy hazmat suit and slide my eyes over to the pocket puff ball inhabited. It was glowing a weak orange-red as if embers were catching into a flame. I stop, my chest rising and falling with the effort I've expended, and look down at the sleeping creature in my pocket. There was no uncomfortable heat as if I was about to burn. All I could feel was a living, breathing creature asleep. Its fir glowed, and I looked up at Fenchurch House just in the distance. I look back to Steve.

"I'm fine," I say. "But when you're feeling better, I got someone I need to introduce to you."

Confused static flashed across the twin monitors of Steve's eyes. I know my comments are noted, but my friend gets back to the arduous process of walking. I looked back to Furball, my new point of focus, and tried to use that against muscle fatigue. I watch how bright his fur becomes as we march up towards Fenchurch House. It's like it's on fire, and I start to squint from the intensity, but as soon as I turn left on Terry Avenue, the intensity begins to fade. The further we get from that building, the more Furball becomes itself again. I'm tired, but my mind is still racing.

What was that?

So much to discover about it. And this was not the right time to ask questions. I just had a niggling feeling that this would not go so well for us. I just couldn't stop what we had set in motion; it was just too important. So I had to keep going with or without help. As the questions began flooding my mind like the speeded-up special effects sequence in a film, I felt the weight of Steve around my shoulders again. Just for a moment, just for a blissful moment, my thoughts have transported me away from the physical forces of the real world. The community center was in sight about five hundred meters away, lit up like a Diwali celebration. It was a celebration, all right. Alien contact of the third kind. Historical even. And I was a witness to it. A pity about the alien invasion aspect of it, but beggars can't be choosers. I don't think it was appropriate, but I was feeling a sense of satisfaction, carrying with it enough feel-good energy that made me straighten up, smile at Steve's bleary-eyed gaze, and march towards the finishing line.

33.

Nikki was slowly being digested.

She had tried everything to free herself from the bubble, but nothing seemed to work. She had enough breathable air for a solar day, so if she sat around and did nothing, she would die of asphyxiation. Instead, the Omni-Seed apparently wanted her to die using her wits and survival instincts. Slowly it was introducing a colorless liquid into the greenish transparent bladder she was trapped in. On analysis, it was an organic acid, and her onboard computer was extrapolating how long the integrity of her exoskeleton would remain to protect her.

The numbers didn't look good.

At the rate it was trickling in, she had three hours before her suit was utterly compromised. With that in mind, there were steps she must take. Nikki wasn't alone in this. The two teams were set up for this reason; as unprepared as they were, they were the only options to save this world.

The Omni-Seed saw her as the main threat and, with one brilliant stroke, took her out of the game. It was only after she was committed to assaulting the building that she realized this was a trap. A ruse she fell for. Nikki was doubtful the seed was even in this building. And that's why she had made this decision. She had not expressed her feelings to Clayton directly because he may have taken it the wrong way, but for a human, he had potential. He took to the idea of extra-terrestrial life existing outside of his solar system as self-evident; he had an enquiring mind that made unusual connections about species that he had never experienced before. Yet, his assumptions turned out to be correct. He was a natural leader and gatherer and was the only one she would trust with access to Uncle's resources.

Clayton was the only one who could end this.

It seemed Ylak Marr would be an inscription etched into the bark of the great Joloba Tree on her planet. A fallen gatherer, revered and never forgotten. Yet, nobody would know she had caused the destruction of a world and deserved to be heaped with shame, not praise. That thought spurred her on as she opened up the console buried in the armor of her forearm and began to transfer command protocols from Uncle to her human friend, Clayton.

34.

I shouldn't be pissed off, but I am. I've just arrived at the community center, and the place is buzzing with refugees who fled their flats or apartments due to the infestations. All of them are scared, all of them with questions. So, of course, I answer what I can. But first, I get Nikki's first aid kit, apply a shot to Steven as instructed, and get someone to watch him while he sleeps. We are definitely not equipped to handle anything more severe than the scratch except for my limited stash of ET meds. Before I came back with Steven, Prescott had been keeping residents calm. I find that out later, but seeing him at the community center without Nikki makes me lose my rag.

I should have handled this better, but what do I know about war and high-stakes circumstances? I'm a rookie trying to manage my own emotions of fear and doubt.

"Where's Nikki?" I ask him after looking around and not seeing her.

Prescott looks tense, and from his body language, he knows this is about to get heated. God knows what he saw out there or how he is feeling. It was just that at this moment, I don't give a shit.

"I waited," his voice barely creeping above the ambient sounds made by the residents.

"What?" My voice is high-pitched and sharp, carrying my incredulity and a shade of disgust.

"I had to leave her. She wanted me to leave her."

It obviously didn't rest well with Prescott either, but showing compassion was the last thing on my mind.

"Leave her where?" I snap, wanting to hear the whole story but not getting the details as quickly as I'd like. "Is she hurt? Is she dead?" I push on.

Prescott steps back from my onslaught, taken aback by my anger. However, he is more surprised than fearful, and instead of matching my immature outburst, he calmly explains.

“I don’t know what to tell you. Nikki didn’t want me directly involved in what she had planned. She told me to get away and regroup if she didn’t get out. She did what she had to do.”

I turn away from Prescott, my head slumps. He is three times my age, and I’m speaking to him like I would my mates. Mom wouldn’t be please with me at all.

Prescott continues.

“Nikki thought the seed was in Runnymede House, but she couldn’t be certain. That’s why she stormed it in the first place.” He pauses, thinking. “She never signaled or contacted me, so I don’t know whether she was right or not.”

“And you didn’t try to find out?” I ask.

“She was perfectly clear on what she wanted me to do, and I did it.”

“We’ve got to go back there,” I suddenly announce. “She could be trapped, unable to reach us. What if she did find and destroy the Seed?”

Prescott sighs.

"She would have found a way to tell us. That was the plan."

"And if she couldn't?" I snap.

"If Nikki didn't stand a chance against these things, what chance do we have? She was the brains, after all. The advanced alien."

I see red again.

"And that's how you fucking see it?" I ask him. "Did you ever consider why she decided to share her secret with us, then turn around and trust us to do this?"

Prescott didn't take long to think about it.

"What choice did she have? There are no rocket scientists on Spikeway Housing Estate, mate. She was desperate."

I shake my head.

"You don't get it, do you. We were chosen, man..." I interrupt myself. Before I say it, I understand the mistake I made.

Why am I having this discussion when the world is on the brink of destruction? Nikki chose me because I'm willing to sacrifice more. Even though Prescott understands what is at stake and his expertise is essential, I just feel that he is too keen about saving his own skin.

Nikki knows she can trust me; she saw something I may not have seen in myself. I look up at Prescott, a mask of self-pity on my face.

“You should have done more man,” I sigh. “I don’t give a shit what Nikki said. You should have done more.”

I turn and walk away from him.

35.

Usually, I'd be fuming after a confrontation like that, but I'm feeling lighter. I am clear. If this is to be resolved, I'm the one to do it. I just can't see how. All I knew is win or lose, I won't be sitting on my arse. I make better decisions on my feet anyway. My mind is racing as I head back to see how Steven is doing when my RPB1, still slung around my neck all this time, starts to vibrate rhythmically. I find a private spot behind some old mobile chalkboards and take a look. A glowing blue line running around the frame of the weapon is pulsing in step with the vibration. It startles me for a minute and reminds me of a mobile phone call. Maybe Nikki is trying to reach me.

It's only when the weapon suddenly turns transparent, and I almost drop it, that I think I understand. There is a compartment nestled away in the stock with something that looks geometrical and spiky. I rub the pad of my thumb over the strange material that makes up the weapon, and the section melts away to reveal the odd object. I shake it out into the palm of my hand and watch the hidden compartment reseal itself. The weapon turns opaque again.

I look at the odd object nestled in the lifelines of my hand. It's about the size of a golf ball and, depending on what angle you look at, seems to be a cube, a sphere, or a prism. In whatever form the optical illusion comes, all its surfaces have protruding spikes of varying lengths moving in and out like small pistons. It feels funny in my hand.

"What is this, Nikki?" I ask the object. "How is this going to help me?"

The object bleeps at the sound of my voice and shoots up from my hand. I look up and around to see where it has gone and feel it slam into the back of my neck. The force knocks me to my knees. What should have been pain is a cool anesthetized feeling with Nikki's voice in my head, calm and reassuring. She is telling me to relax and accept. There is nothing to worry about; it's not permanent. A voice says this like some kind of psychic recording trapped in the confines of my skull.

The pain I'm expecting never comes, just a prick to the back of my neck, numbness, a weight like a mild headache, and the sensation of cold metal on my skin. I resist the urge to touch the foreign object. Fear and curiosity battle each other for a moment, only to be superseded by more pressing considerations.

Another voice replaces Nikki's dulcet tones, and it's old, authoritarian, and wise like a hypnotist's suggestion.

"Link established," it says.

My legs turn to jelly as I slide down the chalkboard to my arse. I can feel my eyes roll into my head and a cinematic reel of images and sounds flash across my mind's eye for what seems like an eternity. Then, finally, my ears pop and the disorientation is gone.

I must have blacked out for a second or two because I wake up with my chin on my chest, my mouth open and drooling, my legs still tented but apart, and my arms hanging on my knees. The accompanying headache is epic. I'm not a pretty picture.

"What the fuck just happened?"

Someone makes a sucking sound somewhere inside my head.

"Keep up, hu-man," the voice I thought I'd imagined in my breakdown sounds impatient. "Ylak thought you were worthy enough for us to co-join, but I'm not so sure."

I stammer out the name I had heard her mention so many times before.

"Uncle?"

I stand at the roundabout and look up at Fenchurch House in the distance. In my left hand, I hold an old birdcage with Furball comfortably tucked inside. My whole body is tingling since I co-joined with the sentient spaceship that is Uncle. I wanted to get Nikki out of the bind she was in, but that couldn't happen. And I was the only option left to fix this situation. I went straight in to rescue the damsel mode, and Uncle wasn't having any of it. Dissent from a juvenile species was out of the question.

The pain he dished out for my insolence is still ringing in my ears. I'm connected to the miserable old shit, and he has the upper hand. And that isn't the only thing. The RPB1 feels different. It isn't just a piece of equipment slung around my shoulders with the power to scare and distract transformed creatures roaming the estate. I have a sense it has an assortment of powerful functions that are now at my beck and call.

"Ask questions, hu-man French, before you start destroying lifeforms."

Uncle startles me because I forgot he's in my head. He continues.

"That's right, I'm in your cranial shell. So, get used to it." His mocking tone is unmistakable, even if his English is stilted.

I think it, and he responds.

"Don't you worry, my language skills will improve by the second while your strategy skills have no hope of improving."

The bastard can read my thoughts, so I have no need to be diplomatic.

"My strategy skills are fine, thank you. You've improved my thinking process by orders of magnitude by co-joining with me. Never knew that would happen, did you?"

Uncle huffs.

"We are not in the habit of sharing our knowledge with species whose technology has not allowed them to travel beyond their star system or develop their extrasensory perception."

"Tough, Nikki thought different. It was that clarity of thinking that allowed me to realize there was a connection between Furball and the Omni-Seed."

"How so?" Uncle asks.

"Can you look into my memory?"

"What do you think I am, one of your puny Exa-FLOP computers? Of course, I can."

"Cool. Well, look into my memory when I was heading back to the community center with Steven and Furball. He displayed bioluminescence that intensified the closer we got to Fenchurch House."

Uncle extrapolates a conclusion from the input at hand, creating a statistical model showing that one in a thousand forced mutations cannot be controlled by the Omni-Seeds influence.

Furball is that one.

Furthermore, it exhibits a trait of bioluminescence when it's close to its creator. I'm proving that theory at the moment. I have Furball comfortably set in a birdcage I found in a storeroom at the community center. Just like the canaries that were carried by coal miners back in the day to detect excess carbon monoxide, I'm using it to detect the presence of the Omni-Seed.

I'm not sure how long I have been standing here staring at the seven-story building whose appearance tonight of all nights is an ominous one. It sits there, its architecture meant to encourage community, instead it sends a cold dark chill up my spine. I shift the birdcage from my right hand to my left. Then take the first step. I'm not alone, I tell myself. Uncle may think our species inferior, but I will do whatever it takes to make this right. I think of Nikki and where she could be, dead or alive. My heart is heavy. I clench my buttocks, my balls, and my jaw and march towards the building.

36.

Furball is like an incandescent light. I gently place the birdcage on the pavement and shield my eyes from the light beam generated by my cuddly friend.

"How you doing?" I wiggle my finger through the bar.

I'm a little concerned about the effect the intensity of its bioluminescence must have on it. But it seems fine, shuffling over to rub its cheek on my fingers. I look up at the apartment building, and the profound silence descends on me. I know what I'm about to face. Uncle has fed me the possible scenarios, but recognizing the Omni-Seed's uncanny flair for strategy and misdirection, I start to wonder what new kind of hell on Earth I'd be walking into. The Seed's creations are wreaking havoc across the estate. Here, on the other hand, is creepily quiet. All the windows are like dead eyes, vacant and dark.

I check my watch.

Three thirty-four.

The power must be off in the whole building, or something else is happening. The penthouse flat doesn't seem to have a problem with power at all as a throbbing rhythmic light pulses in the sea of darkness like a lighthouse. I shift my attention to Furball who is whimpering softly in the cage at my feet.

"It's here, isn't it?" I ask my hairy buddy, but the little powderpuff just continues to whimper and shiver. "We both feel it, I know. But you are gonna stay here, mate. Don't you worry. If I don't come back for you, someone else will. So, sit tight, little one."

I cover the cage with a flannel I have been carrying around to mop up my sweat. I'm hoping this will calm its nerves. Ignoring my pounding heart, I address Uncle.

"Are there any signs of life inside?" Not the kind

of question I would've asked my work colleagues three weeks ago. Now the question is posed to an irascible sentient spacecraft thousands of years old orbiting the Earth.

I pinch myself, but the nightmare persists.

"Life signs are weak for forty-five dwellers. However, two dwellers on the top floor are exhibiting heightened bio signs."

"And the Seed?"

"My scans detect nothing, hu-man French."

For a being of such age, wisdom, and data, it shouldn't have a problem calling me by my first name, not my last. Sentient computer or not, I'm confident Uncle is taking the piss.

"How's it able to do that?" I ask.

"A millennium of adaptation and bioengineer-ing."

"A weapon," I state.

"An old weapon, hu-man French."

"What kind of resistance am I going to face in there?" My bluntness is fear shouting at the top of its lungs, but I have it under control. My new upload has obviously given me the ability to manage fear, or else

I'm not sure I'd be able to do this.

"Scans reveal no adapted organisms. The coast seems clear outside of the hu-man inhabitants."

I'm inexperienced in this, but even to me, this feels hinkey - to quote a term from Thelma off Scooby-Doo.

"The last time you tangled with it, Nikki said it was cunning, resourceful and persistent."

"The organism was hiding in plain sight. It did not announce its presence with attack dogs. It's a Balac'c Tut player." Uncle pauses in my head, and I can feel him rephrase the term. "Chess player. It thinks many steps ahead, but it's vulnerable. It would use any organism at its disposal, and that is where its weakness resides. The Omni-Seed is as strong as its weakest link finding where it's stationed in the whole battle is the key."

I look at the birdcage covered with my flannel, and it resembles those old school Tilley paraffin lamps my mom told me about back in the old country. Furball is throwing off some serious lumens.

The weak link.

For reasons known only to my subconscious and

my newly acquired awareness, my next steps feel right and dangerous at the same time.

"Are you ready, hu-man French?" the centuries-old intergalactic curmudgeon asks.

"I'm always ready," I lie.

Fear can do weird things to the mind of ordinary human beings. I, on the other hand, have become version 1.001 and my upgrade handles stress differently. A reggae tune pops into my head as I look up to the Ice-Cap, I swing the RBP1 to my chest and push into the foyer of Fenchurch House. I find myself reciting the words of reggae artist Buju Banton.

Strange this feeling I'm feeling,
But Jah love we will always believe in,
Though you may think my faith is in vain,
Till Shiloh, I chant Ras Tafari's name.

37.

Ylak Marr wasn't dead yet.

She was waist-deep in digestive fluid and had unsuccessfully tried to ignite a laser welder that powered down on contact with the acid. She swore in English, Perexian, and Slakzan, but none of the expletives gave her satisfaction. She would not expire without a fight. The Omni-Seed would not have its way with Earth without a fight. Her thoughts were on two fronts now. Escape and whether Clayton had successfully received the transfer. Ylak wasn't even sure his physiology could handle the upgrade. Soon they would know because either Clayton would step up and do what must be done, or he'd be another casualty of an impending alien invasion. She hoped he understood that.

All Ylak knew at this point was the connection she had with Uncle was severed, and she felt hollow inside with its absence. Hollow but not helpless. She breathed deeply to focus; her biology required oxygen which her exoskeleton provided, and she was thankful for that. All Ylak needed now was the ability to think. Until such time as her body went into shock and the digestive juices in this bubble ate through her armor, she had some options, and Ylak was cycling through them all, one at a time. Something would work; it had to.

38.

Shadows sliver over everything as I check the floors on my way to the penthouse. All lights are inoperable. I even try messing with the main junction box for the building, but no joy. I'm on floor three, and I'm standing at the entrance looking at the darkened corridor ahead of me. There is a booming bass resonating through the concrete structure all the way from the penthouse to where I'm standing. And yet, it's like I'm inhabiting a bubble of silence that has me jittery. All the apartments are dark and locked shut from the inside. I have an uneasy feeling about this, but I push myself.

My merging with Uncle has done wonders for

how I think and my physical capabilities. My night vision has improved and keeps getting better, and so has my stamina as I run up the steps without a noticeable increase in my heart rate or breathing. And then there's my intuition. I'm feeling things I'm not sure how to interpret, especially the finer distinctions, but I do know what threat or danger feel like. At least the human race has had a millennium to bake that into our collective consciousness. That experience is showing as my enhanced eyesight checks the doors of the five flats on each level of the building - the ground, first and second floors.

Number 33 on the third floor is proving to be the first exception. It's ajar. I blink, thinking it would allow me better focus like a lizard. Lo and behold, it works. A layer tint is removed from my vision, and the scene around me becomes brighter. Number 33 isn't the only door ajar. So are 34 and 35. I know the occupant of 34. Mr. Walliams is a cool dude. I grip the RPG1, still not comfortable with the telepathic link with Uncle, and whisper.

"What's going on behind those open doors?"

He's back at me quickly with an answer I'm not

happy with.

"It's becoming increasingly difficult to gather data within the affected zone. My scans are providing less reliable information for every sweep I make. For the three doors, life signs are barely detectable but unusual."

"Just like the others in the other apartments?"

"Just like the others, hu-man French."

I walk into the landing, not wanting to check the open doors but knowing I must. The tension is palpable, but I know it's an echo from my old programming. My usual signals for fear have been replaced with focus and clarity of mind. All the other unnecessary human baggage have been replaced with a strange economy of emotion that works. I step forward, reaching out to Number 33. The door made from metal and synthetic material feels cold to the touch. The whole atmosphere here feels wrong. I attempt to swing the door wide. The idea is for me to step around it and into the apartment with my weapon up.

It won't budge.

It isn't the kind of resistance that is utterly unyielding like a rock or something solid. Instead, the obstruction is flesh and blood. The nozzle of my RBP1 comes up just as the former residents stepped out of their flats in unison like grotesque puppets. I shuffle back my stomach lurches, my heart pounds against my rib cage, and the skin of my scalp erupts into goose-flesh. Mr. Walliams and his neighbors do not look good.

Whatever the Omni-Seed had done to them, the transformation is horrific, almost spiteful. I have seen the change on other animals, but these subjects were not given the due care and consideration from the Seed's sculpting knife. It was a rush job or a sign of the disdain it holds for humankind. They still walk on two feet, swinging two arms, and I'm thankful for that. Everything else about them is grotesque. Their red eyes bore straight through me, and their snarls are feral and focused.

The residents lope like predators, sniffing the air, their disfigured bodies sinewy savagely powerful and ignoring me for the time being. In the scintilla between my thoughts, the RPB1 is crunching numbers of range and power. I feel like I'm not entirely in control as I target the creatures. I let off five bursts of energy from my weapon in an arc, diving to my right as I do. It's a weird sensation controlling the weapon with my thoughts but one I quickly get used to.

I hit what was once Mr. Walliams and his neighbor, flinging them both into a concrete pillar. The third creature is athletic and fast, ducking my initial salvo. I may have missed it, but I keep tracking it in the cramped surroundings. They may be ugly, but they move with speed and gravity-defying agility. Taking a circuitous route to rip my head off, it bounces off the wall and barrels into me as I release two more blasts from my weapon. Both shots go wide, dissipating against the concrete ceiling. I have never been hit by a car before, but I'm guessing it would feel like this.

I'm thinking cracked ribs and bruised muscles, but just for a moment. I take a breath, hurting all over and allowing my spinning head to settle. I'm on my back as the rabid neighbor comes for me again. It's so close, I can't get enough space to fire at it. I propel myself backward, frantically glimpsing the stirring shapes of the others I had dispatched earlier. I can't handle all three at once, and that thought is a cool expression of fact. The reality of this lands on my chest and stomach, knocks the air out of my lungs and begins to relentlessly pound me with its powerful hands. I squirm and thrash.

Trying to match its power is useless, but I manage to prop the RBG1 under its chin and proceed to pry its head up. Its hands are digging into my arms and its jaws snapping like a shark, its breath a rotten vegetable pong that wafts into my face. I turn away from the smell, but I keep my arms extended under its neck. All this time, my fingers are kept busy on the weapon. Once I get a better grip, and I can't stand the pain in my arms any longer, I let go. Its head dips for my throat, and I swing the RPB1. Its temple connects with the butt of my weapon, but satisfaction only comes when I swing my weapon around again. It connects sweetly near the jaw, sending it careening sideways. This is my opportunity.

I spring up, firing two energy rounds into the resident. I pummel his head, swing around, and light up the other two who are regaining consciousness. To say I'm buzzing is an understatement. I can feel every bruise, every gash. My lungs are working like the bellows for a steam train, but I can do more. I'm tingling all over, and the sensory inputs are acute. If class 'A' drugs are anything like this, I can understand the appeal. I look around at the carnage like a lone Shaolin monk who has dispatched his enemies. Pushing through the doors ahead of me is my next move to get to the fourth floor.

Uncle interrupts my short-term plan of action.

"Well done, hu-man French. It seems that you Neanderthals have managed to develop a precognitive power in your evolution. Your intuition was correct. The Omni-Seed is here."

"What makes you so sure?" I ask.

There is a pause, which I'm going to believe is done for dramatic effect.

"All the transformed organisms are heading for this location. The Omni-Seed is worried. If they reach you before you get to it, all is lost."

My shoulders slump.

"No pressure then. How much time have I got?"

Uncle shows me the timer. My muscles tense, my heart rate spikes with anticipation. I burst through the doors and into the stairwell, looking up to the gloomy top, thinking this optimism cannot be good for me.

39.

It was only when Ylak thought she had tried everything that an insane possibility darkened her thinking.

She was desperate.

The digestive fluid was up to her chest, her exoskeleton had begun bubbling as the crystal-metal alloy was losing integrity, and like a creeping rot, her onboard systems were failing too. She wouldn't suffocate but would be dissolved by the molecular acid in this floating digestive tract. Ylak was exhausted from her effort and may not have come to this suicidal idea if she hadn't drifted into a protracted version of her sleep cycle.

The answer was in the structural components of her RPB1.

Her weapon had one backup power cell built into the frame. It was super-insulated and stabilized in a zero-containment field. Outside of its environment, it was unstable, and that's what Nikki depended on. The power cell had a duration of two Kronuts - which were two revolutions of her homeworld around their binary star. Plenty of fusion energy to last many missions and constant use while traveling between star systems.

What if she could overload it, just enough to breach the bubble without flattening the whole building and the surrounding neighborhood? Her exoskeleton would provide her with rudimentary protection as the power cell exploded and then shut itself down. She would have to get it into the containment field before the runaway reactions would cascade out of control. That explosion did not bear thinking about. She did the calculations in her head, and from what she could see, there was a 70:30 chance of success.

Uncle would have made sure the numbers added up. She didn't have his raw computing power or his wisdom to call on now.

It was all on her.

She shrugged as if saying, what the hell. These human mannerisms were addictive.

With that decision made, Ylak meticulously began stripping her weapon and carefully retrieving the thumb size micro-fusion reactor.

’m heading towards my clean-up job

40.

I look and feel like shit.

Uncle had been right; the Omni-Seed is throwing everything it can at me. I'm stupidly concerned about subterfuge while it's intent was on removing me from the chess game permanently. With both my hands on my knees, I'm breathing hard. I'm at the IceCap, outside of the penthouse suite, catching my breath and trying to reconcile what I did to get up here. Running the gauntlet of residents I knew before they were turned to these mindless berserkers was unsettling. These same residents I had hurt and possibly killed to get to where I am now.

My heart is heavy and my gut is sour; it feels like

I've lost too much, and there are considerable consequences to come if I do not stop this thing from spreading into the world at large. A surge of panic quakes through me, making me raise my head and look at DJ Greggo's front door expecting the worst. I may not look it, but I'm pissed. No polite knocking for me tonight. Gentility had been abandoned from the first floor. I'm tired, and I'm beginning to doubt I can do this. Without the merge and Uncle, I'd be dead. The thought of it makes my knees weak, but I try not to focus on the enormity of it. I've got a job to do for Nikki, the estate, and possibly the world.

Stepping back from the ornate front door, my fingers dance over the RPB1 in a pattern that changes the weapon's power levels. A thought materializes in my head. I brace myself, and the weapon fires, sending a stream of energy in ever-expanding circles that slam into the door, crumbling it like paper and then ripping it off its hinges. The music and the heat issue out of the apartment, carrying the memory of my last encounter with the DJ.

I should have known something was unnatural about the place. The music is reggae as before; the sweet-smelling tropical aroma is even more attractive. However, this time the pull of the apartment is more sinister. The Omni-Seed is in there. I can feel it thriving off the Jamaican root's music, the heat, and plants. It loves music. The vibration, the frequency. Maybe somehow the reggae and heat provide it with the energy it needs or stimulate it in some way. Maybe this is the closest it can get to an ideal environment. I wonder how long DJ Greggo has been under its control.

I barge in with my weapon raised, my situational awareness on alert. The apartment is like nothing I could have imagined. It's a greenhouse filled with exotic and strange plant life thriving in this urban habitat. I cautiously prowl down the corridor. My boots are cushioned by a bed of vegetation. The walls are teeming with vines and creepers that I do not recognize. The door is festooned with garlands of exotic and alien plant life. From the floor to the walls and onto the ceiling, flora burst through every surface it was able to. There are rooms to both sides of me, but I'm compelled to keep dashing forward.

What I want is ahead of me and nowhere else. I just know it.

The walls vibrate from the reggae beats. It feels wrong for such uplifting music to be hijacked by this thing. A soundtrack of hope and redemption is being fed through the leaves, stems and flowers by an entity that is the antithesis of all that. And I can almost see the plants in the act of growing, or is it an optical illusion from the vibration. Actually, I'm not seeing things. The plant vine slivers serpentine towards me, strikes at my ankle, then strikes again. My legs buckle, and I feel my body begin shutting down; my heart is racing. I stumble to my knees, and my head is swimming. I'm losing consciousness until Uncle intervenes somehow.

"Those thorns contain neurotoxins, deadly to your kind, hu-man French. But you're far more than human after the merge. So, I have triggered a biological response. The feeling will soon pass. In the meantime, adjust your RPB1 to maximum and purge the route ahead."

I'm genuflecting with my head bowed. I'm drooling a bit, my weapon pulsing a subdued light that keeps more vines at bay. Finally, the feeling does pass, and I stand up.

I do as I'm told.

I skip back, use my thoughts and fingers and fire bursts of energy from my weapon. The thorny stalks explode into a brackish sludge that splashes the walls and ceiling. I release another sweeping wave from the RPB1, and the wall of vegetation forming between me and the lounge liquefies. I make an awkward dive into the lounge before anything else tries to stop me. I roll back to my feet, clumsily ready for anything. Uncle needles his way into my brain again, showing me the progress of the menagerie of mutated creatures that are honing onto my position. They are in the building and climbing up the sheer sides. My eyes take in the room without movement of my neck. What I want isn't in here.

It's out there.

DJ Greggo stands on the balcony, his back against the railings, his eyes wild, his mouth mumbling like a kind of demented lullaby. And that makes sense because in his arms, lovingly held close to his chest and being rocked gently to and fro, is the Omni-Seed, throbbing like a living nuclear bomb.

41.

Uncle is feeding me an avalanche of information, and I think my human senses are approaching overwhelm. But tucked away within the frailties that make me human are the added powers given to me that are uninterested in my limitations. They know I'm capable of more.

I absorb the onslaught of information in my stride.

Now I know when some of the mutations will reach the sixth floor, I know how much time I have to neutralize the seed. I even know how much power is required from my RPB1. What I don't know for sure is how my attack will affect DJ Greggo. Will it rip him apart violently, render him unconscious or gently disassemble him, molecule by molecule? I can't hesitate; there are questions to ask but too much at stake. I strum the RPB1 like a guitar and feel it alter its emission as it compensates for the targets in front of it. I feel like I'm being pulled in four different directions at once as the forces from the particle beams impacts my body as it rips from the alien weapon in my hand. When the light show is over, DJ Greggo and the Omni-Seed look unscathed, unconcerned.

"Fuck," I spit.

I give them another sweep of deadly particle beams.

The quickly fading spherical outline of a forcefield, invisible and powerful, evaporates before my surprised eyes. The DJ's attention outside of the Omni-Seed in its arms is directed skywards. He looks beatific, as if he is expecting the second coming, not of the Messiah from heaven, but of something less forgiving, something from the gaping depths.

Uncle is parroting in my head. He wants me to cycle through different frequencies and keep testing the integrity of the force field around them.

There's not enough time, and I don't have a quick fix. So, I shrug obstinately and begin my charge. I'm sprinting through the lounge at full tilt. More vines try to snare me, but I'm going too fast. The balcony is drawing closer, I feel the chill air outside, and it dawns on me. A sudden realization.

It's a pickup.

As I hurtle from lounge to balcony, a dark flock of flying creatures above me are descending. They want to airlift the seed to safety. Airlift it to a new base of operations so it can decimate the planet. Head down, shoulders squared, I'm going at a furious clip avoiding furniture and the animated creepers trying to snare and trip me up. My only focus is the DJ and what he holds. My mind is absent of consequence; it feels like Uncle himself can't get to me. My singular focus is the DJ and the Omni-Seed.

My eyes narrow, my legs pumping hard as I prepare to impact with the force field. I grit my teeth in anticipation...

There is nothing.

And in a split second, I understand. The force field only reacted to energy weapons. A good old-fashioned shoulder charge from a low vibratory object goes unchallenged. I run right through it like it's a barrier only in my mind. I smash into DJ Greggo with a crack, my momentum taking him, the Omni-Seed, and myself over the edge.

42.

I launch off the six-floor balcony and into the heart of darkness. My brain is shutting down as panic overwhelms me and gravity pulls me in for a bloody embrace with the concrete below. I begin to scream against the air rushing past me, filling my eyes, my nose, and lungs, but it's short-lived. Time slows as a sense of calm overtakes me. A part of my human self wants nothing more than to live, but the part of me that merged with Uncle, the alien intelligence many miles above me, is satisfied with me dying if it means destroying the Omni-Seed. It's for a greater good, it reasons. I'm not sure I'm cool with that. I haven't lived yet. I'm not sure I like how this is going to end.

43.

Ylak sprinted with her ears still ringing from the explosion that had freed her and destroyed the sixth floor of Runnymede House. The offending fusion reactor was safely back in her weapon, and as she moved like a gazelle through the streets towards the beacon of Fenchurch House, she thanked her exoskeleton's weak force-field for saving her life. If she hadn't been told by Prescott where Clayton was, the menagerie of mutated creatures marching like rats from the Earth tale of the Pied Piper of Hamelin towards Fenchurch House would have been a giveaway. She flew past the snorting, mewling and grunting mutations that ignored her as they focused on one thing.

The Omni-Seed.

It had shed its veil of secrecy and in desperation was broadcasting its location for all to see.

Ylak didn't have Uncle's resources to magnify her senses, so she had to rely on her innate Magnoxian sensory array. Uncle's Mimicry Programming had made it difficult for her to call on her inborn sensitivity – it was supposed to make her human disguise more real. But the contained fusion explosion that had helped her escape her captor had also caused her less than acute human senses to slip. She reached out to the building with a broad wave of psionic energy and sound. What bounced back was a chaotic and confused parcel of auditory and mental impressions that were focused on the top floor.

She looked up, still moving fast, and amidst the jungle of sensations she was sifting through were the distinctive signature of the RPB1 being discharged. Ylak skidded, changed direction in mid flow and was pointed to the building's entrance.

Above her head came the scream.

Clayton.

A Magnoxian perceived time differently from humans, her thought processes were quicker and so were her reactions. Ylak swung her RPB1 from her back and gripped it with both hands. Her third appendage would have been helpful as she fought her violently bucking weapon as it rapidly synthesized elements being produced inside itself, combining it with the air around, creating bucketloads of yellow spongy material that stuck against the buildings and the ground.

She looked up again just to make sure she had positioned herself correctly and watched the two humans and the Omni-Seed fall from the sixth-floor apartment building in a kind of time dilated dance. The fall trap looked like it had been produced by a giant Zervon spider, but it didn't need to be neat, just effective. She awkwardly smiled down at the ball of fur who was wide-eyed in its cage, and then modified the output of her RPB1 with a thought. She watched as Earth's gravity pulled the two bodies into the sticky tangle, abruptly stopping their descent.

Clayton was thrashing his arms and legs wildly like he couldn't believe he was alive. Hollering like he had scored a goal in one of Earth's many competitive pursuits. Due to the velocity of the fall, the Seed rolled some fifty feet away from them. Clayton stepped over the curled up DJ Greggo who, other than his clothes covered in yellow gunk, looked like he was having a bad dream, mumbling to himself. Clayton headed towards the Seed but hesitated and shrunk back when the stampede of creatures on his left were also beating a path to their creator. Clayton raised his RPB1 on weak knees, but Uncle checked him.

"Human French, do not engage," the sentient computer demanded. "Ylak has a plan. I know it."

Ylak Marr did have a plan.

She could sense the mutated creatures closing in on the Seed's new position. The flying things were already hovering around. Another wave of leathery, scurrying creatures the length of her arm was attacking her with sharp claws and teeth. And that was one of many creatures gnawing madly on what remained of her battered exoskeleton. Clawing and ripping at any gash or rent, eager to taste the soft flesh inside of the hard exterior of her shell. She flashed off what she could and focused the weapon on the Omni-Seed.

Steadying herself, calming her breathing, her

Magnoxian senses locked on to the extraterrestrial Seed, but its minions would not allow it. In minutes, Ylak was overcome with a writhing, squirming, screeching mound of mottled grey, leathery skin, and glistening shell. She could see nothing but felt the weight of the creatures on her. With Zen-like poise, Ylak directed her thoughts to the RPB1 and held her breath. A sound like the growl from a giant Krendax grew with the expanding energy bubble from her weapon with Ylak at its center. The force pinned her to the ground and radiated outwards, crackling like an electrical storm. The vermin closest to her disintegrated instantly, and the rest exploded outwards in a bloody cloud of mangled pieces with a cracking boom.

When the smoke cleared, Ylak was on her knees; her exoskeleton was in tatters, and thin streams of smoke issued from it. She looked unstable on her feet, but her intention was clear. With her hands unsteady she speared the Omni-Seed with an intense particle beam from her RPB1 that wrapped it in a colorful traction cloud, lifting it up and blocking its connection with its creations.

Suddenly, the encroaching menagerie of genetic

oddities that had been bearing down on her paused. As if a switch had been flicked in their heads or a set of confusing messages sent to them. Those creatures with luminous eyes blinked in confusion, antennae twitched questioningly. For some, tongues flickered, tasting the air for answers, and the ones who despised the light, multi-legged, venomous, repulsive organisms merged back into the darkness.

Ylak looked over to Clayton, who was walking towards her with his hands over his ears, picking his way through debris and viscera. He threw his arms around her when he got close enough.

"You did it," he raved. "Fucking hell, we did it." Clayton paused, then stood back. "Where were you? What took you so long?"

"Being digested," Ylak said.

Clayton feigned understanding with a shrug.

"Okay then."

"I think you better tell Uncle we need clean up," Ylak said. "And a transport for the seed."

"I can do that, can't I?" Clayton asked, sounding pleased and surprised.

"You can," she said.

Clayton’s smile got wider.

’m heading towards my clean-up job

44.

Who would have thought clean-up after an alien invasion would take so much time, organization, and stress. A week after the confrontation with the Omni-Seed and its minions, most of the evidence they had ever been here was captured, stored, and the rest destroyed. Truth be told, Uncle and Nikki did most of the heavy lifting in the guise of government contractors cleaning up after some chemical spillage - that always seems to work. Automatons were sent down from the mothership securing live specimens and biological material.

I had to act as chaperone for the AI as they went about their business. I was deflecting questions from some residents amazed at how advanced our technology had suddenly become and the worry that robots were taking over the world. Little did they know this was the least of their worries. The Omni-Seed was transported to an ultra-secure habitat that I hoped was harder to break out of than its first enclosure.

Spikeway Housing Estate suffered property damage - 6th Floor Runnymede House was gutted, the massive subsidence of Percival House, the disappearances, and the casualties. People I know died here, and I'm not about to forget it. Amidst the tragedy, I realized I have a knack for extra-terrestrial pest control - if that ever becomes a thing. Not something I would ever want to have on my CV unless I'm excited about a padded room and straitjackets. I, for one, am proud of what I've become. It may be a skill I'll never have use for again, but I'm cool with that.

It's some minutes after ten at night according to my smart watch. For now, I have my hands back in my pockets, my fingers playing a piano sonata on my thighs. I'm trying my utmost to look cool; I'm just not doing an excellent job of it. We, humans, are an expressive race. Blame it on our simian ancestors. I can deflect the emotions with humor, as I have always done in situations like this. It's just that this time it feels disingenuous after all we've been through. Nikki deserves the real me, the annoying unfiltered me.

I push my hands a bit deeper into my pockets, looking at a vast expanse of parkland, while I act as if I can see the invisible scout ship stationed somewhere ahead of us in the darkness. Nikki stands quietly beside me, a mystery I can never hope to understand, and on the other hand, she is a sister in arms and a friend. A good friend.

"What now?" I ask, still staring at the open land.

"I must continue my journey home and document my adventures for my gatherer brothers and sisters."

"Does it ever end for you? Will you ever hang up your space boots?"

Her laugh is short and melodious. It's a beautiful thing that needs more time in the world. But it frightens the shit out of me anyway. I don't think I ever saw her laugh before, ever.

"This is my life, Clayton. I chose this while you were forced into this life because of me."

"I had to; this is my home, but it's over and done.

I just wish you could …" My voice trails off, my wish sounding pathetic and needy as it leaves my lips.

Nikki smiles.

Her human inflections are getting good.

"We won the battle but not the war," she says.

I'm looking at her with my mouth open and lips trembling.

"What are you saying, Nikki?"

"There is a high probability there will be more threats to your planet, more threats to your community. You will have to keep your people safe."

I'm almost relieved with her trademark bluntness. It's the message I have an issue with.

"Wait a minute," my heart is racing, my head is spinning. "Are you saying there are more of them, more Omni-Seeds?"

"We still haven't ascertained how this particular species reproduces. However, they propagate their species for an organism as maliciously intelligent as this one, it cannot be underestimated. The Seed will have prepared for what just happened to it." She places her hands on my shoulders. "But it's not prepared for you."

"Nikki I…" I start protesting, but she hugs me

close. She smells divine. Her kinky hair tickles my nose; I feel her breasts pressing on my chest, her hips on mine. She kisses my neck and I hear her sigh.

"I'm not supposed to have been here," Nikki says. "Or interacted with your species, but I would not, I could not have left you to die. Now my human form wants to stay."

"I want you to stay," I say taking her hand and kissing her fingers.

Nikki looks away.

"Listen…" I try to interject again as my world shimmers like an unexpected squall you get in some hot climates.

At first, I think I'm losing my marbles, then I'm confident I'm not. I look at Nikki. I'm still holding her hand, and for the first time, I can see who she really is behind the illusion of being human. She is spectacular in her true form, and strangely enough, my feelings towards her don't change when she reveals the real her. I hold onto one of her arms as she continues to walk away from me towards her spacecraft. My hand slips from her spindly arms to her stork-like hands, then her three small digits, and then between us is space. She keeps walking, lighting up the darkness with her glow, but turns back to me as if a thought has struck her.

"I have left some things for you and Steven in the Bat Cave, and a star to watch over you. You'll be more than prepared, and you are ready. Just remember you'll never be alone, never."

The scout ship sparkles into tangibility, and Nikki discards her human form once and for all. The craft opens up to receive her, and she enters. Before she disappears from sight, Nikki turns and waves. Then she's gone. I stand, watching the scout ship camouflage itself. This time I can see the outline. I can hear it too. A tingling sensation engulfs me as my eyes sharpen, and my ears pop like I'm ascending from Homo sapiens to something slightly more.

You are ready, Nikki's words remind me.

Ready for what?

"Did you think merging with Uncle would not change you?" The words resonate in my head, making me jump. An itch on the inside of my skull requires scratching that can only mean one thing.

"Human French, Earth-orbiting pest control unit." The words in my head have a fresh note to them but carry a familiar irascible pedigree.

"How much longer must I wait for your first order?" Uncle 2.0 asks.

I smiled broadly, even as tears roll down my cheeks.

<u>Don’t Forget to Review</u>

A review is like oxygen for my books. I live for them; I love them and I'm so appreciative of readers when they take the time to share their opinions and support my work. Thank you for finishing the book, I hope you enjoyed it and if you did, help me to spread the love.

ABOUT THE AUTHOR

Anton Marks first novel began a trend of bestsellers that would transport readers to the ghettoes of Kingston Jamaica in **Dancehall**, futuristic London – **In the Days of Dread**, government agents in **Bushman** and the futuristic world of vice in – **69**.

In 2013 Anton rolled out the beginnings of a *Charlie's Angels* type supernatural thriller called **Bad II the Bone** and the second in that series **Good II be Bad**. He also began a young adult sci-fi/fantasy series under the name Anthony Hewitt. The first book **Joshua N'Gon: Last Prince of Alkebulahn** and book 2 **Joshua N'Gon & the Battle for St. Augustine** released in 2020. To cater for his more concise work Anton has created a short story line called Urban Fantastic Shorts. In this collection are **Messiah**, **Chauffeur**, **Omega Point** and **Pest Control**

www.antonmarks.com

Printed in Great Britain
by Amazon

48154636R00175